"It's illogical."

"There never is anything rational about mutual attraction," László replied silkily.

Suzanne knew he was trying to seduce her for reasons of his own, far beyond desire. She lowered her eyes. "I'm...I'm not inviting sex!"

"Unfortunately, you are," he returned lazily.

"You keep your distance! We're on opposite sides of the fence. You're blackmailing me to get what you want and it must be obvious that I despise you!"

"Really?" László mocked.

DESTINY awaits us all, and for Tanya, Mariann and Suzanne Evans—all roads lead East to the mysteries of Hungary.

Tangled Destinies

As Tanya arrives in Hungary for her younger brother's wedding, her older brother, István lies in wait after four years. He's the only man she's ever loved—and he's hurt her. But what he has to tell her will change the course of her life forever.

Unchained Destinies

Editor Mariann Evans is on a publishing mission in Budapest. But instead of duping rival publisher Vigadó Gábor—she is destined to fall into his arms.

Threads of Destiny

Suzanne Evans's attendance at the double wedding of her sister Tanya and her brother, John, presents a fateful meeting with mysterious gate-crasher László Huszár. He's the true heir to a family fortune and he has a young family of his own. He is about to make sure that his complex family history is inextricably linked with hers, as all the elements of this compelling trilogy are woven together.

A Note to the Reader:

This novel is the third part of a trilogy. Each novel is independent and can be read on its own. It is the author's suggestion, however, that they be read in the order written.

SARA WOOD

Threads of Destiny

DESTINY
BOOK
3

Harlequin Books

TORONTO • NEW YORK • LONDON
AMSTERDAM • PARIS • SYDNEY • HAMBURG
STOCKHOLM • ATHENS • TOKYO • MILAN
MADRID • WARSAW • BUDAPEST • AUCKLAND

ISBN 0-373-11802-3

THREADS OF DESTINY

First North American Publication 1996.

Printed in U.S.A.

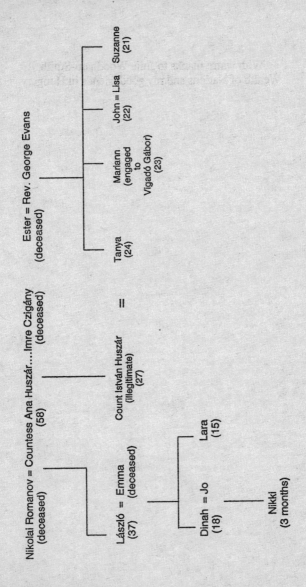

Ester = Rev. George Evans
(deceased)

Tanya
(24)

Mariann
(engaged
to
Vigadó Gábor)
(23)

John = Lisa
(22)

Suzanne
(21)

Nikolai Romanov = Countess Ana Huszár....Imre Czigány
(deceased)   (deceased)
                    (58)

=

Count István Huszár
(Illegitimate)
(27)

László = Emma
(37)   (deceased)

Dinah = Jo
(18)

Lara
(15)

Nikki
(3 months)

With warm thanks to Julia Woodham-Smith,
Wealth of Nations and my good friends in Hungary

CHAPTER ONE

'THAT man—there!'

'What man, where?' grumbled Mariann.

'He's gone! *Again*!' Suzanne's face fell.

'Paranoid,' her sister declared scathingly.

'He *is* following me,' insisted Suzanne. 'Everywhere I turn, he's staring at me, like...' A little shiver rippled down her back. No, she thought hastily, appalled at what she'd almost blurted out. She couldn't say 'like a messenger from hell!' Her sister would take her to the Funny Farm. '...like I've sprouted a purple nose!'

The two sisters giggled. 'To tell the truth,' mused Mariann, 'he's probably struck stupid by the way you look tonight, Sue. What's happened? Been at the face pack again?' she teased.

Suzanne gave Mariann a withering look, but she did feel different. Almost beautiful—which was unusual. Her two gorgeous sisters had always attracted the lion's share of male interest up to now. She'd invariably ended up with runty cubs and the odd hyena.

Tonight had been unsettling, the way she'd drawn men's attention. It was partly due to the guy himself, she realised. His ink-jet eyes, that wonderful slow, sexually charged look, had made her heart race and her body tingle with an unaccustomed excitement because she'd felt so intensely desirable and utterly feminine. Desirable because his gaze had told her so...

Mercifully, her common sense surfaced. 'I think champagne happened, Mariann,' she said wryly. 'That plus emotion; having my sister *and* my brother getting married on the same day, *and* knowing that *your* wedding's due soon, is enough to make anyone dizzy.' She adopted a casual tone. 'Umm...just in case you see this guy, find out who he is——'

'Idiot! There are hundreds of hunks in this crush! Describe him,' said Mariann fondly.

Suzanne flushed, trying not to sound too interested. 'I've only seen his head above the crowd——'

'Tall, then. What else? Has he got any hair?'

'Lots.' She ignored her sister's flippancy, recalling every detail of the man's image without difficulty. 'Jet-black, smoothed back and very sleek. Strong features, Hungarian cheekbones, a tan I'd die for...' She saw her sister's smirk and decided to forget the foot-long eye-lashes and the sexy curve of dark hair in front of his ears that she'd itched to touch. 'Actually, it's his eyes that you'll notice first.'

'I'm looking for a guy with eyes.'

'When you see them, you'll know what I mean,' said Suzanne quietly, still haunted by their extraordinary intensity. 'They're...' She gave a half-embarrassed laugh. 'You know how level-headed I am, but even I can see they're compelling. Mysterious.'

Her brow furrowed. That wasn't entirely all. The fascination she felt lay in the fact that nothing had been constant in the alarmingly sinful blackness of his eyes, apart from the sparkling mercurial dance within them, coupled with an arrogant challenge as though he wanted her to go over and ask, 'Who are you?' So she hadn't.

'Sultry,' she went on thoughtfully. 'Sort of sleepy—except that sometimes it seemed they were piercing right through me——'

'Lawksamussy, dear!' Mariann patted her hand. 'How many eyes has this poor guy got? It *is* the champagne.' She sighed, her slanting, hazel eyes mirroring those of her sister. 'Drink a gallon of coffee and lie down with a wet towel on your head, Sue! You're quite wonderfully muddled! I must tell Tan—I've never known you to be so totally off your trolley before!'

Suzanne laughed ruefully. 'So would you be,' she protested, 'if a stranger tried to scramble *your* brains with an egg-whisk. I think he must be either a hypnotist practising on the unwary, or deeply short-sighted. In either case, he's...dangerous,' she added soberly, remembering the wicked promises that had been directed at her like well-aimed arrows.

'Just the sort I like,' grinned Mariann. 'Go find him. Have a great time!' She rolled her hazel eyes comically and left.

Immediately, Suzanne furtively scanned the ballroom for a sight of the elusive stranger, determined to pin him down and satisfy her curiosity. To her deep disappointment he was nowhere to be seen. Feeling distinctly unsettled, she decided that she'd do better to forget the guy and begin thinking about the crucial meetings she had the next day.

So she left the wedding party and walked slowly into the moonlit garden, the floating panels of her silk ballgown drifting behind her like gossamer on the grass. She felt the breeze lift her long, straight hair and automatically pressed it flat again, smoothing it into order.

Ahead gleamed the great lake that stretched to the beech woods. As she came closer she drew in her breath. A figure stood silhouetted against the sheet of moonlit water.

Beneath the thin silk of her bodice, her heart began to thud loudly. Drat! The guy she'd been talking about! She'd know that powerful head even from the back. It had become emblazoned unforgettably on her mind. Seeing it now made her feel quite nervous. Illogical, of course. Absurd.

Overwhelmed with an urge not to be seen—at least till she was perfectly composed—she stepped quickly behind the cascading branches of an old shrub rose. Its ethereal white flowers shimmered in the breeze and swamped her in a tantalising perfume as her fine-boned face lifted to see what the man was doing.

Apparently nothing. But there was sadness in the angle of his head and an anger—or perhaps frustrated despair—that revealed itself in the repeated clenching and unclenching of his hands. He wanted to hit someone, to lash out in blind rage and it was the kind of rage that hurt, very deeply.

Her breath shortened. He'd looked so sardonic and unassailable before, and she wondered what he was desperately trying to hide and why he should be so interested in her when there were scores of beautiful women to choose from.

Suzanne shifted her naked shoulders impatiently at her ridiculous fantasies. The reason his back was so tense was probably indigestion! She smiled at the thought. Maybe, she decided, with her usual practical turn of mind, he'd come out to clear his drunken haze. Or to escape from his nagging wife. Or even to agonise over his stomach ulcer.

Whatever the reason, he was very still. Despite the conventionally tailored dinner-jacket he seemed to fit in with his surroundings, and she had the impression that he felt more at home out here than in the confines of the castle, magnificent though it was.

Imperceptibly, his body tautened as if he was listening—perhaps to the rustle of animals in the undergrowth, the soft murmur of the rustling beech leaves, or the night birds... She felt her heart lift, hearing the piercingly sweet sound of a nightingale. It reminded her instantly of long summer evenings spent in her Devon home she loved so much.

'Why are you hiding from me?' he asked, suddenly whirling around. 'Not your usual direct, confrontational style, is it?'

Suzanne gave a little strangled gasp at his softly spoken question. Her feet had made no sound on the tightly mown grass and yet he'd spun lightly on his heel to face the flower-laden branches of the rose which concealed her.

'Afraid of me?' he persisted, with quiet mockery.

'Of course not!' But she was. And sheepishly she emerged from her hiding place, feeling rather foolish, too. 'I didn't want to disturb you,' she explained hastily. 'It looked as though you were chewing over a problem and needed to be alone.'

'I *was* thinking,' he drawled, all tension wiped from his body. Despite the deep shadows from the giant clipped yews that concealed the details of his face, he looked relaxed. 'I was also waiting for you to appear.'

Her disbelieving peal of laughter rang out into the silent night. 'How clever!' she said with a grin. 'I've never met a thought-reader before!' Seeing his frown, she added, 'I can't see how else you'd know I'd come out here.'

He made no effort to conceal his interest in her, his extraordinary eyes sweeping over her with a calculating male approval that made her body soften as though he'd melted it. Alarmed, she stiffened every muscle before he interpreted her response incorrectly. This wasn't a man you could tangle with and come off unscathed. A kiss would mean seduction. Seduction would mean... She frowned, jerking back from the image of Paradise and concentrated on what he was saying.

'...so I didn't need a crystal ball to guess that you'd follow me,' he was murmuring laconically. 'I knew I'd sent enough messages persuading you to search me out.'

Suzanne's mouth opened and shut again in astonishment. 'The truth is,' she said coolly, annoyed by his assumption that she ran after guys who raised black and wickedly expressive eyebrows at her, 'I had no idea you were here. I came out for a stroll because I've got a lot on my mind——'

A grin slashed the dark anonymity of his face. 'I know,' he interrupted enigmatically. 'And now,' he added with an infuriatingly smug satisfaction, 'you have me to think about as well.'

The guy had concrete skin! He needed serious squashing. 'Why on *earth* would I do that?' she asked coldly in simulated amazement.

'Because you won't be able to stop yourself,' he replied in amusement.

'I'll try,' she promised drily, rather amused herself at his blatant nerve. 'Oh, I'll *try*!'

And then he began to stroll towards her, walking with the grace of a natural athlete, the lithe limbs flowing like liquid. Into her normally matter-of-fact mind came the vivid image of the wild ponies cantering joyfully on the moors at home. He moved with the freedom of someone who rarely knew the restriction of four walls; who acknowledged no man-made boundaries to his world; a guy with a glorious sense of freedom which he indulged shamelessly, like the unfettered ponies.

No nagging wife had ever chained him to the kitchen sink. Nothing so commonplace. And that ox-strong body looked as if it could eat or drink anyone under the table without any side effects. So no indigestion, no ulcer. What then, she wondered curiously, had made him so tense when he'd thought himself unobserved at the lakeside? It had almost seemed as though he was steeling himself in preparation for an unpleasant task, and she regretfully had to fight back the urge to ply him with questions.

'Don't bother to try. You'd be wasting your time,' he said smoothly. 'You won't stop me from making myself the centre of your life: the guy you think of when you get up in the morning, the guy you dream of at night.'

The extravagant claim made her laugh. It was too ridiculous! 'I'm sure this is your best chat-up line,' she said wryly, 'but I suggest you'd do better to try your luck elsewhere. I don't have any time for guys who think they're Adonis reincarnated.'

'You'll make the time.'

So confident! she marvelled. His back was to the silver light, his face still in the shadow of the forbidding yews. But she could see the glitter of his eyes as his slow gaze ranged over her body. Its raw male hunger made her unusually conscious of the flimsy material between her nakedness and him. And suddenly she was deeply, enjoyably aware of the sensual way the silk caressed her warm skin. Pleasurable sensation was taking over her workaday world and she wanted to lift a hand to contain her galloping heart, but dared not draw any more attention to the tightly fitting bodice. He'd studied that part of her body for too long as it was!

She felt the soft petals of a rose between her fingers. The intensified fragrance drifted to her nostrils and she discovered to her chagrin that she'd unwittingly crushed a defenceless bloom. The stranger chuckled as though he found her absent-mindedness encouraging and she frowned at him, summoning up some sense from her trembling, beautifully assaulted body.

'Don't hold your breath,' she said tartly. Ironically, she was holding her own breath because he was moving forward now from the shadows and she found herself completely thrown by the expression on his face. Magnetic, she thought, her pulses racing. And deliberately so.

Without any regard for social propriety, he stood within nerve-tingling inches of her, his head angled so that the shafts of silver light fell on the aristocratic bone-structure of his face. Suzanne drew in several steadying jerks of air from her bewilderingly crushed lungs, afraid of his intentions.

And then she saw that the black hair had threads of silver above the temples and she realised he was more mature than she'd first thought, despite the youthful movement, the young man's passion that lurked in those secretive eyes.

And finally, like it or not, she was driven to ask the question that had hovered on her lips for so long. 'Just— who—are you?' she croaked huskily.

'László,' he murmured, imbuing the name with soft, seductive sibilants. He took her hand in his and lifted it, bowing his dark head, his lips a hair's breadth from her alarmingly quivering fingers. When he shot her a look from beneath his black brows, his eyes were twinkling in sinful amusement. 'I am an Angel.'

'Devil,' she corrected breathily in a weak joke. But meant it. How else, she thought in dismay, could any normal man play havoc with her insides?

He smiled as though in confirmation. 'If you like. In either case, I'm the answer to all your prayers,' he mocked.

In confusion, she drew her hand away. Flirting wasn't something she indulged in and it made her feel uncomfortable. 'As far as I remember,' she said levelly, with an attempt at a casual shrug of her pale silken shoulders, 'I put in a request for peace on earth and a balding banker.'

He laughed in delight then dropped his eyes. They'd been sending unwelcome signals of a rather intense hunger to her. The dark lashes flickered on his prominent cheekbones—a true Slav feature, along with the straight black brows and the finely chiselled mouth that hinted at extreme sensuality. She felt a little wobbly and sought a reason.

Champagne, she thought, remembering her earlier excuse to her sister. Please let it be that! she thought. It had flowed like water and she wasn't used to such luxuries. Her legs felt boneless suddenly. Hiding a rueful smile, she reached out her small, delicate hand to rest on the low wall behind her for support. He saw the gesture and looked pleased so she hastily explained, with a small laugh. 'I'm a bit giddy——'

'Yes. I thought you were,' he drawled.

Flushing at his meaningful tone, she struggled to knock this conversation on the head and to run—no, walk casually!—back to the ballroom. The strains of a slow, dreamy *lassu* came from the ballroom where her sisters must be dancing; Tanya with her new husband, Mariann with her fiancé. It was time she joined them before the romantic night softened her brain into a sloppy blancmange.

'It's the non-stop dancing,' she said, all on her dignity. 'My legs are shaking with over-exertion.' His expression told her that he didn't buy that. 'And I'm full of bubbles!' she continued in desperation. 'I need a quiet moment to recover. So, if you don't mind, perhaps you'd go and dance to that gypsy music with someone who really appreciates dominant guys who come on strong,' she suggested bluntly.

'That's not gypsy music. Can't you hear that it lacks raw emotion? It's Hungarian, with a dash of tourist,' he answered cynically.

Since he was determined not to budge, she began to walk beside the lake and realised too late that she was moving away from the house. Nervously she hoped he wouldn't think she was encouraging him. 'I thought the orchestra were all gypsies,' she said irritably, for the sake of something ordinary, anything, to break the increasing tension. 'They're wearing gypsy costumes.'

'You're dressed like an innocent. But who knows what hell-fires lurk beneath the flimsy silk that's struggling to cover your breasts?' he argued, his eyes burning into her pale, swelling flesh above her bodice and she willed her hands to hang at her sides and not to betray her agitation by clutching her bosom like a frightened virgin—which she was. Before her apprehensive eyes, his mouth grew softly sensual. 'I might look conventional,' he said huskily, knowing he must look nothing of the kind, 'but what cruelty and what secrets are concealed beneath this Milanese tailoring? What wicked schemes am I dreaming up, even now, while I walk beside you, enjoying your extraordinary beauty? And what lies would both of us be prepared to tell to save our skins, or to project an image of how we look to the world?'

She was shaken. That hadn't been a casual line of thought. It was almost as though he was warning her about his intentions. Afraid to involve herself with him, she decided it would be safer to ignore his extraordinary remarks.

'The music sounds genuine to me,' she said huskily and bristled at the sardonic smile that swept his lips into a wicked curve and taunted her for being a coward.

'Authentic gypsy music is never heard by any outsider,' he said gently. 'Besides, it needs the open air for it to come to life. A room throttles its spirit.'

Intrigued despite herself, Suzanne considered that solemnly for a moment as they walked silently across the closely cut grass. Floating across the softly lit garden, the lilting cadences of the violins became sharper, more painfully emotional as the group got into its stride and let rip with a deep, Hungarian passion. Touristy or not, it did sound better under the stars.

'Yes,' she conceded slowly. 'Indoors it sounded like a Viennese operetta. Here, it's...' She hesitated, unnerved by the man's satisfied growl.

'Yes?' he prompted, in a disconcertingly smoky voice.

'It sort of joins the air,' she finished lamely. It also seeped into her bones and filled her head like an intoxicating drink, weakening every inch of her with its seduction, but she wasn't going to tell him that. The thought was startling enough, without voicing it.

He didn't laugh. She would have been mortified if he had. 'Given the opportunity, it will pervade our entire bodies,' he husked. 'And make us helpless because it calls to something primitive and reckless within us all.'

He felt that too. She groaned inwardly, not wanting him to lose control of his emotions. She stumbled; his hand reached out and cupped her elbow and then dropped away again. But she'd felt the dry heat of his palm and her body felt shot to pieces from the current of sexual electricity that had passed between them. Frightened by the intensity of his emotions—and his apparent decision to direct his attentions to making a pass at her, Suzanne managed to lift her shoulders in a casual gesture.

'I suppose it has to go somewhere,' she said, attempting to sound amused. But she felt confused, because the fateful combination of the music and László was definitely doing something odd to her out in the garden, reaching parts she'd rather were left dormant.

Something—someone—was casting a spell on her. Too many people getting married, too many lovers around! she thought ruefully. The whole day had been a fairytale; the bridal procession for the dual weddings of her sister Tanya and brother John; the picturesque village church, its wooden interior bright with folk paintings; the lavish picnic in the castle grounds; the pageantry of the glittering banquet and the ball afterwards. No wonder her feet seemed to be floating above the ground. It wouldn't do! She was supposed to be the sensible, down-to-earth one in the family! Time to land on solid ground again.

Coward's way out.

'I wish you'd go,' she said curtly, stopping dead in her tracks and letting her irritation show. 'I'd like to be alone.'

'Face to face with a challenge and you don't like taking it up?' he murmured provocatively.

Her mouth thinned. 'You're not a challenge,' she said with a firmness she didn't feel deep inside. 'Look, if you're determined to deny me some privacy,' she added, with a toss of her head, 'then I might point out that, as a relative of the man who owns this land, I have a greater claim on this bit of the garden than you do.' Her hand waved vaguely at the banks of orange blossom, pouring out their heady scent.

'I wouldn't count on that,' he growled softly and his expression hardened like stone.

Her huge hazel eyes searched him warily. 'My sister married Count István Huszár today. This is his estate. My brother manages the Castle Huszár Hotel——' she began in stiff reproof.

'I accept that you have quite a strong connection with the land.' To her astonishment, the extravagant mouth thinned and a film of pain briefly dulled the brilliance of his eyes. 'It's natural that you should imagine I have less right than you to be here.'

He said that as if it weren't true—which was impossible. And she wondered what he was trying to suggest. There was something odd about his manner, as though beneath that apparently suave exterior he resented István for owning the castle. She wasn't sure why she should think that, except perhaps for the faintly contemptuous curl of his lip when she'd spoken István's name, the unconscious way he'd planted his legs apart when she'd mentioned her right to be there and the possessive sweep of his gaze whenever he'd scanned the landscape.

She shivered. Someone had walked over her grave. Seeing his hard, cold eyes on her, she pulled herself together quickly. 'Well, I can hardly credit that you've bought the estate from my brother-in-law on his wedding-day,' she remarked sarcastically.

'As if I would! He and your sister would be homeless then, wouldn't they?' he answered. The smooth, silken tone turned to gravel. 'And so would István's mother,' he growled. 'The tragic countess.'

He hated them all, she thought suddenly, paling with the knowledge. But why? 'What do you know about them?' she asked warily. An unnamed and irrational fear clutched at her heart. She must find out. 'And what——?'

'Are you intending to live here?' he broke in, totally ignoring her questions and scowling down on her. 'One big, happy family?'

'No,' she said curtly, a need to find out more about this guy and an ingrained politeness prompting her to add; 'Hungary is beautiful, full of wonderful people—and I've enjoyed my time here immensely, but I love my Devon home too much ever to leave it permanently.' Her expression took on a far-away, wistful look, easing out the lines of worry. Widecombe-in-the-Moor. Soft green hills, ancient woods, tiny stone villages and peace. She'd never, ever want to settle anywhere else.

'Then it's even more extraordinary that you speak Hungarian,' he observed, his sharp eyes on her. 'Not a bad accent, either.'

'Thank you,' she said, grudgingly delighted by his praise. Carefully skirting around him, she began to walk back, and he immediately joined her, moving so close to her hip that he was in danger of treading on her skirts. 'I took a crash course in the language,' she said, wondering how she could turn the conversation back to István. 'I need it for my new business. I'd learnt Russian at school and that seemed to help—also the fact, perhaps, that my late mother was Hungarian.'

He showed no surprise, which rather disappointed her. She was proud of the speed with which she'd picked up the notoriously difficult and unique language—but then she had the motivation, of course.

'Maybe your roots are stronger than your English up-bringing,' he said quietly. 'Our blood has a way of making itself felt.' Suzanne looked at him, surprised by the slight tremor of emotion in his voice but he continued before she could comment. 'And now you practise by chatting to the Hungarian guests at this *lavish* double wedding. So much happiness in one family,' he drawled.

Suzanne stiffened. Somehow he managed to sound as though he wished them ill. Her hands began to shake and she gripped her skirts. 'We've all worked hard for what we have,' she said nervously. 'No one gets anywhere without effort.'

'That's true,' he agreed drily. 'It was quite an effort for me to gatecrash this wedding.'

'You're a gatecrasher?' she asked, stopping in utter amazement. He didn't look like one—in fact he displayed an assurance and a sophistication most men would envy. So it was inconceivable that he'd stoop to gatecrash a party. The back of her neck prickled. Perhaps he was an uninvited enemy, who'd come to cause trouble. 'Why come to the wedding?' she asked sharply. 'Given a choice, most men would rather have all their teeth out!'

'Oh, food, fun, to meet people.' His eyes flickered and narrowed. They were never still, but constantly watching every detail of her expression, each movement she made, and she felt disturbingly *naked* as a result of his constant watchfulness. 'I thought it would be interesting to see the estate and its owner.'

Her heart sounded loud in her ears. There had been a wealth of meaning in his bitter tone and in the grim bleakness of his expression. 'To make trouble?' she asked huskily, her eyes huge with anxiety.

'I lived here once,' he said, his voice flat and unemotional.

Suzanne gasped. 'In the castle?'

'I was born in it,' he said shortly.

'Born here! That's amazing! No wonder you had the urge to gatecrash and make a sentimental journey!' She ignored the sardonic curl of his lip that suggested he didn't know the meaning of sentimental journeys and thought rapidly. Since the countess had been in residence all her life—and had no living relatives—he couldn't be a nephew. 'Was your mother a guest here when she was pregnant or something?'

She'd been mentally calculating that Hungary would have been under Russian dominance at the time of his birth. His mother must have been a friend of the countess. Or a friend of the countess's hateful husband. Forgetting the wisdom of keeping a distance from this man, she paused and looked up at him, searching his face for clues to the mystery, knowing she wouldn't rest till it was solved.

The dark eyes glittered briefly. 'My father lived in the castle. I left when I was still a baby.' His hand briefly caressed her head and she took a startled step backwards. 'The moonlight makes your hair look like a sheet of black silk,' he murmured, switching effortlessly from the factual to soft seductiveness.

'Does it, indeed?' she said frostily. 'I *knew* you must be short-sighted. My hair is actually chestnut in the cold light of day.' To her amazement, her voice was husky, as though his velvety words had affected her. Her finely drawn brows met in concern over the slender bridge of her nose, the shadows darkening her eyes to a glowing chocolate brown.

'I'm not short-sighted,' he said softly. 'Everything about me is operating at one-hundred-per-cent capacity and is firing away on all six cylinders.' Suzanne swallowed, knowing full well what he included in that claim. He flashed his white, even teeth in mocking amusement at her reaction. 'I can only say that your hair is the most beautiful I've ever seen, that your face has a luminous quality and your eyes would——'

'Put the stars to shame?' she suggested croakily, furious at the falseness that laced his words. He was teasing her, she thought angrily. 'Stop flirting,' she muttered through her teeth. 'I don't fall for blarney.'

'You weren't getting any,' he answered soberly.

For a long moment, their eyes locked and she read the truth. This wasn't a casual flirtation, born of politeness or boredom. He really did find her attractive. No, she had to be honest; he had strongly sexual intentions. There was an element of intent about his expression and a stark, raw need that had no business in those languid black eyes.

She flipped up her head and her straight fall of hair swung heavily around her bare shoulders. 'Back off. You've gone far enough,' she said levelly. It was her Nanny-knows-best voice and had made men cringe before as if she'd delivered a slap and sent them to bed with a bowl of porridge. It had no effect on him.

'We're going to go a lot further than this,' he promised confidently. 'All the way, in fact. And I must confess, I'm relieved you've interpreted my interest so accurately. You've saved me at least twenty minutes of small-talk and gentle persuasion.'

'You arrogant——!' Her neck lengthened as she drew herself up angrily to her full five foot seven. And found his eyes melting irresistibly into hers. It was a moment before she could trust her voice to be steady. What a gall he had! 'It didn't need much interpretation,' she snapped. 'Your signals have been so powerful that I'm surprised no one's picked them up on the BBC World Service. I know there's a tradition of bridesmaids being available for a little romancing at weddings, but that doesn't apply to me. If you're after an evening's amusement, you'd be better off chasing moonbeams.'

'I don't think so. You're perfectly aware of what there is between us,' he told her softly, completely ignoring her rebuke.

'Yes—too short a distance,' she countered crisply. 'I intend to make that half a mile.'

'Stay,' he ordered, his eyes melting into hers. 'Let me explain the plans I have for you.'

'Explain them to the fish in the lake,' she muttered. 'You have as much chance of landing one of them.'

Disdainfully she walked away, discovering to her irritation that she was having to force herself to break the threads that had held her tethered to the spot. Grimly she strode on. So she was fascinated by him. Attracted. Drawn by his hints of mystery, the thrill of some unknown danger. She knew that he had dishonourable in-

tentions and yet the urge to throw caution to the winds
and prolong their meeting was unbearably strong.

He was laughing, the sound reverberating in his deep
chest and finding disturbing resonances in hers. 'We'll
meet again, Suzanne, depend on it!' he called after her,
while she frantically pressed her fingers hard against her
emptied lungs.

Her pace quickened till she was striding angrily along
the greensward, her long skirts flying behind her. She
knew he was watching her and her naked back and
shoulders were icing under his gaze. In that laugh had
been a sinister undertone, a threat of some kind. She
stumbled, gritted her teeth and carried on, walking faster
and faster till she was out of breath and faintly slicked
with sweat in the warm night.

CHAPTER TWO

REACHING the brightly lit terrace, Suzanne felt her common sense return. What an idiot she was! Enter dark stranger, collapse of feeble heroine! For a moment or two she paused to catch her breath and gather herself together. His air of looming menace and the hint of secrets had been purely to intrigue her and she'd almost fallen for the clever ploy. How many women had he mystified into bed? No guy had made her forget her purpose in life before and persuaded her to think of romance, of love, of the pleasures of the flesh she was deliberately foregoing. That László had done so annoyed her intensely, wounding the pride she felt in maintaining her single-minded ambition.

She'd given herself eight years. At the end of that time, she meant to be running her own business—successful, of course—and could *then* begin to consider a partner. Any earlier than that and she would not have achieved her lifelong dream, nor would she be old enough to have enough sense about men.

After all, she knew nothing about them. Her sheltered vicarage childhood had been dominated by the close relationship with her sister-friend Mariann, her idol, the most beautiful woman she'd known. Her elder sister Tanya had always seemed a mother figure, though Tan's love for István had certainly changed her into a radiantly lovely—if slightly bemused—bride. Suzanne's mouth curved into a fond smile. Tan deserved all the happiness in the world after her troubled life.

But for her, well, mused Suzanne, men had always been a disappointment. The boys at school had exasperated her with their talk of football and larking around. Kids, to a man. Even the guys at Medway School of Art had seemed immature to her and they'd become

21

bored with her serious approach to life, her blind obsession to carve her own way alone, unhindered by relationships.

The smile became a grin. Young men behaved like idiots, getting drunk, boasting, competing. If you gave them half a chance, they dominated you, did something weird to your knees by making them weak, softened your heart and interfered with your own personal aims because theirs always had to come first—her sisters' guys excepted, of course!

Despite the alarming rash of wedding bells in her family, she vowed that she wouldn't be diverted from the passion that had held her since she first learnt to sew a seam.

Perhaps it was due to being the youngest. But she desperately wanted her own achievement, her own independence. She was going to do this her way!

A figure passed her, as silent as a walking ghost. László. A pair of glittering eyes, narrowed like those of a man used to combating the smoke of a campfire, flicked in her direction briefly, leaving her with the impression of sardonic amusement.

'Taking a rest? Gathering yourself together?' he murmured.

The whole of her treacherous body had sprung into life. 'I'll gather you with steel hawser stitches if you don't leave me alone!' she said frostily, wondering why he made her feel so female.

'Ah. Edgy,' he murmured, pleased. Leaving her bristling at his perception and yet blushing in shame from her dreadfully snappy remark, he crossed the broad terrace, pushed aside the draped wedding garlands over the French doors and disappeared into the crowded ballroom.

She groaned. Grinding her teeth in frustration, she stemmed the impulse to stride after him and demand to know why he was trying to unsettle her and what his link was with István. It was patently what he wanted, but she was going to put him out of her mind. After a while, she decided he must be well into the throng so she moved to the ballroom doors and tried to focus on the dancing couples.

Odd, his claim to have lived at the castle. He certainly hadn't been a servant's child, not with that autocratic ego! She must ask István about him if she could get near him. Her eyes fell fondly on her brother-in-law, surrounded by well-wishers.

'Sue!' Tanya had grabbed her arm urgently. 'I've been looking for you everywhere. Little Lindi has dropped strawberries on to her dress. What should she do?'

'Eat them,' she said absently.

'Ask the countess for the traditional herbal remedy,' came the all-too-familiar sexy tones of the mysterious László.

'Thanks!' Tanya laughed and leaned confidingly towards the man who stood half hidden by the heavy brocade curtains. He was just inches from Suzanne's shoulder and she felt the cool whisper of his breath over her skin and her stomach plunged at the way her body tightened up in response. 'Normally my sister's the most reliable and sensible person in the world!' went on Tanya affectionately. 'We always go to her for solutions to any practical problems. Tonight I think she's got something else on her mind.'

'I think you're right,' murmured László, his mouth unfairly sensual.

Suzanne tore her eyes away from its inviting softness. 'I'm thinking,' she muttered stiffly, 'about stitching people up.'

She flung a meaningful glare at László and grimly slid away, escaping through the crowded ballroom and out into the quieter, less congested hall where she leant in relief against the mirrored wall. It was wonderfully cool to her burning back and she sighed, letting her breath fill her lungs again.

'Feeling hemmed in?'

She felt her hackles rise at the softly caressing voice and its underlying laughter. This was becoming a nightmare. Would the man never leave her alone? Chill prickles cascaded down her spine as she turned a haughty

head, but her face was bewilderingly hot, her hands
clammy, and in her resentment she scowled crossly at
the man standing by a full-size replica of a posing huszar.
Which, she noted with a frown, looked oddly like László.

'Needled,' she said coldly.

'You're avoiding me.' He picked an iced bon-bon from
one of the fluted ice-bowls and bit into it reflectively.

'I'm relieved you've interpreted my lack of interest
correctly,' she said, parodying his earlier remark.

'You're only delaying the inevitable. You must have
realised that I want to talk to you, very badly, and that
I probably have a good reason for doing so.'

Her solemn eyes studied his. Talking wasn't on his
agenda. Even she could see that. 'What reason?' she
muttered ungraciously.

'I can think of several.' He smiled faintly and
swallowed the sweet sorbet. Suzanne's eyes were riveted
to his moist mouth. 'Take a look at yourself.'

Her glance flicked rebelliously to the full-length
mirrors across the hall and she did a double-take. That
wasn't her—it couldn't be! She was plain and uninter-
esting, preoccupied with making others look beautiful
but quite indifferent to the way she looked. Besides, what
was the point? She didn't want to attract anyone. Neat,
clean and simple was enough.

When she'd checked briefly in the bedroom mirror
earlier, it had been with the professional eye of a dress-
maker assessing the way her skirt hung, not for any personal vanity. But tonight, by the flickering candlelight,
she realised that she could almost have been described
as striking.

'What do you see?' asked the devastatingly sexy voice
in her ear.

'A woman being harassed.' Despite her sharp reply,
she kept looking, riveted to the reflection. The straight
sheet of her dark chestnut hair fell from its central
parting around her ivory-skinned face. Sparkling light
from the crystal chandeliers and a warm glow from the
natural candlelight gave her simple hair a rich and
flattering sheen.

'Look again. Objectively,' he chuckled. It was a nice sound. Her eyes slanted to his and he gave her a long, slow look which increased the rhythm of her heart to the speed of a fast and wild csárdás dance. 'Not at me. At yourself,' he said gravely.

She went scarlet and stared ahead, unable to avoid her reflection. She cocked her head on one side. She looked thinner than she remembered. But then, she'd been rushing around lately because she'd resigned from her job making costumes for Glyndebourne opera house and had been working far into the night to check her finances for her elaborate plans. Now the bones of her face stood out stark and angular like a model's, her over-large mouth fashionably full and pouting, a reckless scarlet against the pale skin.

And the dress, lovingly made, lent a wanton air to her body that she'd never intended. All she'd done was to fit it perfectly. Not a bad shape! Quite womanly. No, sexy; the globes of her breasts were shimmering as they rose and fell with her quick, shallow breath... Yes, she thought reluctantly, she understood his interest. Carefully she avoided looking at him and fiddled with her hands. She was disturbed enough already.

'I've looked,' she said dismissively. 'Nothing's changed in my attitude towards you. What you want is of no interest to me at all. Go and chase some other woman,' she said in desperation when he didn't budge an inch. 'Men are not part of my design for living! You're irritating, not intriguing,' she lied.

'I said earlier I was the answer to your prayers. I might not be balding, but I could do a great deal for you.' The tip of his tongue moistened his lips and she swallowed at the rush of sexual tension that small gesture engendered. 'My interest is alarming you?' he murmured.

'Don't flatter yourself,' she said scathingly. 'My world consists of paper patterns and scissors, threads and cotton reels, warehouses, gorgeous materials and balance sheets. I can't squeeze a man in there as well. Ask anyone around here who knows me; I have a purpose in life and if I'm to achieve it, I can't take time out for the Adam and Eve bit.'

'Adam and Eve? I was thinking more on the lines of——'

'May and September?' she suggested waspishly, with a meaningful look at his silvery streaks in the night-black hair.

But he smiled. 'Eve and the snake.'

'Incompatible,' she declared levelly, and recklessly, driven to desperation by his persistence, decided to go further to discourage him. 'Surely even you could see that, at the hint of any link between us, your friends would accuse you of cradle-snatching!'

He didn't even wince. 'And yours will, I expect and our relationship will be difficult, but who cares when there will be so many benefits?' he said in a husky undertone. Suzanne felt a quiver of fear run through her. How certain he was! It seemed cut and dried in his mind that they'd get together and be the censure of everyone they knew! She frowned and made to leave. 'Go if you wish. But turn, and I'll be there,' he murmured, softly sinister. 'Speak, and I'll answer. Listen, and you will hear me breathing; think, and I swear I will be in your thoughts.'

That was true already. Shockingly, she felt herself vibrating because he was near, thrilling to his voice, every fibre of her body longing to feel his touch. The drift of his soft breath sent a shiver of delicious pleasure through her but it was nothing to the charge of electric energy that passed between them. He felt it. She felt it. And... Her panic-stricken eyes noticed people staring. They could see it too!

She gripped a table beside her and let the cold Carrera marble draw her concentration away from the compelling urge she had to succumb to his advances by flinging herself into his arms.

This night of love, the fairy-tale atmosphere and the champagne had a lot to answer for, she thought ruefully.

'This is ridiculous! You're suffering from delusions!' she said coldly. Yet she sensed that there was more to this than a strong sexual attraction on his part. He looked so...knowing. Her pulses fluttered, broke rhythm, intensified their beat. 'Cause me any more trouble,' she continued in a rasp, her eyes searching the hall wildly for someone she knew, 'and I'll find a bouncer——'

'You can't have me thrown out,' he reasoned, unperturbed. 'There would be a terrible scandal and you would never forgive yourself.'

'A—scandal?' Her nerves danced tattoos. She'd been right. 'Why?' she asked through dry lips.

'I'm a relative.'

She blinked, not sure she'd heard that right. 'A relative?' she repeated stupidly, unable to grasp what he meant. 'Of mine?'

'By marriage.' Arrogantly sure of her attention, he glanced up at the quietly melting huszar and touched its smooth thigh. 'I'm related to Count István.' She heard the steel in his voice, saw a cold glitter of hate in his eyes and was afraid. This pursuit of her had been no accident, no sexual whim. He meant her new brother-in-law harm, she was sure.

'Impossible!' she scoffed, on firm ground at last. 'I know his story. Everyone does. István is the only child of the countess and her lover. The rest of the family, including her Russian husband, are all dead.'

'You know nothing. István knows nothing.' The dark eyes flashed with scimitar-blade lights and a grimness claimed his erotic mouth. 'The countess, however, is another matter,' he said huskily.

Again that hint of anguish. Strung taut with tension, Suzanne felt his hurt and knew there was something deeper than hate that drove him to pretend this link with the Huszár family.

'Nonsense! You're making this up. There is no relationship,' she said coldly, her logical mind finding the obvious flaw, 'or the countess would have invited you! It's clear you must be unwelcome——'

'As unwelcome as a corpse at a wedding feast,' he agreed sardonically. 'The countess will be devastated to know I even exist.' Something close to pain settled in his eyes. But it was a dangerous pain. One that demanded retribution. 'That's why we're going to come to some arrangement, you and I,' he said huskily.

'We certainly are not!' she denied, suddenly afraid. Nerves clawed at her stomach as a feeling of dread overtook her mind.

'First we'll bargain. I might agree not to announce my presence to the family, if you promise you'll listen to a rather interesting proposition I have for you——'

'That's out of the question!' she gasped. She pulled herself together. They were in a public place. He couldn't do anything. 'I'm not interested in any proposition made by a gatecrasher at my brother-in-law's wedding!' she grated. 'I think you'd better go before I get you thrown out! You have no right——'

'But I do,' he insisted quietly.

Suzanne inhaled angrily. 'Rubbish! We'll see what rights you have. I'm going to find István, tell him you're here and let him heave you out the door. And I will watch with pleasure and cheer him on and wave flags!' she finished belligerently.

He shrugged. 'As you please. Tell him. Ruin your sister's happiness if you must,' he said in a low tone, and, while she stood in dumb astonishment, he strode across the chequerboard tiles to the library door as though he had the right to go anywhere he chose.

Suzanne felt her body drain of energy. Tanya's happiness? What did he mean? How...? Her breath came rushing out suddenly and she realised she'd suspended her breathing because of the softly savage threat. And it was because he'd been so confident, so absolutely *sure* of himself, with that know-it-all carriage of his magnificent body, that she'd instinctively believed every word he'd said.

Stupid. She looked down at the palms of her hands with a frown, realising they were wet with sweat. There were beads of perspiration in the deep V of her cleavage, too. But she had to settle this. She couldn't risk hurting Tan for the sake of a few minutes facing up to a ruthless bully.

Half stumbling, she ran to the library and flung open the door. He was sitting in István's favourite chair, reading one of the leather-bound books, his long legs stretched out comfortably, perfectly at ease and smiling at her as though she were some servant girl he'd summoned to his noble presence.

'How could I threaten Tanya's happiness?' she demanded hotly. His gaze rested thoughtfully on her heaving breasts and she shrank back for a moment before her anger took over again and she forced herself to call his bluff. 'You're lying! If you were a relative as you claim, you'd be welcomed with open arms,' she argued, her eyes flashing sparks.

'Go on,' he taunted huskily. 'Think why I might be received with fear and loathing.'

'Perhaps because you're a very unpleasant man,' she snapped.

'Naughty!' he said softly, the mobile mouth alarmingly sensual. 'Very, very provocative. And very, very unwise, if I may say so, to annoy me. Who knows what I might do to your life and to your sister's?'

Slowly she walked towards him, fighting for a clear head. It wasn't easy. Not with those velvet black eyes stripping her to the bone, dancing on her body as though he were contemplating the most intimate caresses ... She gulped and came to a sudden halt.

'You're suggesting you pose a threat,' she said with some success at sounding calm and composed. 'That means you believe you know something about István or the countess. An unpleasant secret from the past...'

'Yes?' he drawled.

Feeling sick with dismay, she stared down at her trembling hands. The thought was too awful to contemplate. After long, hard years of unhappiness and poverty, the countess had been reunited with her beloved son István and life had taken a turn for the better. And István—he'd worked so hard ...

Her eyes flicked up. 'I know!' she cried triumphantly. 'You're pretending that István is an impostor!'

He burst out laughing, baffling her completely. 'He is the countess's son,' he said, between brandy-rich chuckles. 'The DNA tests proved that. The authorities would never have permitted the re-sale of the land to him, otherwise. Besides,' he murmured softly, a heart-breakingly bitter twist to his mouth that made Suzanne wince for him, brute though he was. 'It's a poor mother who doesn't recognise her own child.'

She felt an incredible sense of relief. He wasn't going to pretend that István was a con-man and there was no danger that the countess's world would come apart. István and Tanya were married at last and could forget the anguish of the past that had separated them with such cruel consequences. They'd been through a lot, but she was sure their love could withstand anything now. They were made for each other. Nothing could hurt them, not even some rattling skeleton in the Huszár cupboard. Together they'd cope with this threatening guy.

Calmly she lifted her chin and seared him with a blast from her ice-green and chestnut flecked eyes. 'My family is very close,' she said calmly. 'We support each other all along the line. The countess is now part of our family; so is István. I know them well enough to be certain that neither of them would do anything dreadful. I respect them all and have the highest regard for them. If some-one's treated you badly, if a mistake *has* been made, and you have a complaint, I'm sure they'll correct it.'

'You can bet your sweet life they will,' he said lazily, slamming the book with a gesture of finality.

But there had been an imperceptible change in him. The muscles had become taut and beneath his heavy eyelids smouldered angry fires. She considered the predatory mouth and sucked in a suddenly hollow stomach.

'What do you hope to gain from them?' she asked huskily. He was making her hot and dizzy with his in-dolently stroking gaze, each fractional flutter of his thick lashes jerking her nerves into a more heightened state. 'Money?' she suggested hoarsely. 'A job?'

He lifted an interrogatory eyebrow. 'You're fascinated,' he purred. 'Ready to talk, then? And to listen?'

Before she could answer, the door-handle rattled. She swung around to see a giggling Mariann slowly heaving open the heavy door with one red-tipped hand and towing Vigadó behind her.

'Oh! Isn't that typical?' complained Mariann with a theatrical sigh. 'You try to find somewhere private for a quiet cuddle with your fiancé, only to discover your kid sister in the way!' She smiled fondly at the startled Suzanne. 'You won't find Mr Miracle Eyes here, Sue! He's too busy looking mysterious and sultry and compelling and sleepy to read books too!'

Suzanne shut her gaping mouth and wrenched her head around. He'd gone! 'He was here!' she exclaimed. 'Mariann, he was here and he's...'

'Vanished. Hon, are you OK?' her sister asked in concern. She rushed forwards and put her hand on Suzanne's brow. 'You're awfully hot——'

'I'm hallucinating,' Suzanne said, forcing a joke. 'Or—how old do you have to be for senile dementia?'

'Older than twenty-one,' grinned Vigadó. 'Why don't you go and watch the folk dancing and keep my Lindi company? You'll love the costumes. Might give you some ideas.'

'And you and Mariann can—er—talk,' she said with an understanding smile. Behind her came the sound of a softly closing window. The hairs on her neck rose. László was creeping around like a thief in the night. As jauntily as she could, she made her way out, waggling her fingers in farewell to the couple behind her—who were probably already wrapped in each other's arms, she thought wryly.

And she stood nervously arm in arm with her father and Vigadó's daughter Lindi, watching the troop of folkdancers in their traditional costumes and trying to keep an interested smile on her face. Any moment now, László might reappear and make some ghastly announcement. True or false, her frail father was in no fit state to cope with the high drama that László's disclosure threatened.

Unusually, she was taking little professional pleasure in their broderie anglaise blouses and the cut of the huge puff sleeves, or the cleverly layered starched petticoats, romantically caught with ribbons. All the time the multicoloured skirts whirled, the little flowered waistcoats twisted this way and that in the wedding dance, she worried about László's claim that he could wreck Tanya's happiness—an act which would affect all of them deeply.

She looked over to where her dearly loved sister stood nearby, secure in István's arms, and a pain shot into her heart at the love between them.

In the back of her mind, she knew with a sickening feeling that László's threat wasn't fanciful. He wasn't a young man on the make, or playing a silly game. There had been a lot of hidden anger and resentment behind the cynicism. But more to be feared was the searing hurt that would drive his anger to awesome lengths. This wasn't a guy who'd do things by halves. He'd made it clear that he wanted retribution and retribution he'd get.

A dreadful foreboding began to make her restless. Why had he approached her? Why not István himself? Perhaps, she mused, he was wary of confronting the powerful count, and saw in her, the youngest sister, a woman who would be the most vulnerable, the most easily manipulated.

Perhaps she might have been shaken by his deliberately mysterious approach. OK, so her head had been turned by his extraordinary sexuality that he'd directed at her with the expertise of a man with dozens of seductions notched up on his bedpost.

But now she had time to recover, she'd prove that she was every bit as tough as the other two Evans girls. After all, they'd all inherited their mother's tenacity of purpose, her deep sense of duty.

For the moment, she'd delay reporting him to István. Just in case. But next time she met László—as intuitively she knew she would—she'd confront him and demand to know what he was hinting at. He'd been on the brink of saying something when Mariann had appeared and for some reason he hadn't wanted to be seen. She stored that away. It might be useful.

'I'm a little tired, darling girl.'

'Are you, Dad?' she said gently, guilty that she hadn't noticed her father's wilting manner. 'I'll come up with you. Your bedtime too, Lindi,' she said with a warm smile, and the little girl ran off happily ahead of them.

'Your Mum would have liked this do,' her father said wistfully, as they wove through the guests to the grand staircase.

'Dearest Dad, you did love her so,' she whispered, hugging him tight.

'God give you love like mine,' he replied huskily.

Her emotions overcame her and she accompanied him to his room, fussing that he had everything he wanted and reminiscing with him for a while. At least, she thought in relief, if anything *did* happen now, her father could be shielded from it.

To her annoyance, she found herself furtively looking around as she walked along the corridor, as though she feared László's appearance and she found to her dismay that she could hardly stop shaking. It was like waiting for Armageddon.

'Sue? Are you better?' came Mariann's voice.

'Oh, yes, much,' she lied cheerfully.

'Vigadó's reading a bedtime story,' confided Mariann, shifting Lindi's strawberry-stained dress over one arm. They walked down the stairs together with Suzanne only half listening to her sister's chatter about Vigadó's daughter. She had other things on her mind far more worrying. And then Mariann pinched her arm. 'Don't look now, but I'm sure I've just seen your elusive admirer, ogling you fit to bust!' she whispered conspiratorially.

Suzanne stiffened and met a pair of devil-eyes across the hallway. László was back—and judging by the way he looked, with a vengeance.

'Don't be daft,' she said, managing a tone of sisterly scathing. 'He's looking at you, Mariann. Men always do.'

'Not with Vigadó around!' laughed her sister. 'Heavens, Sue! The guy's everything you said and more! *Gorgeous*! And he's positively *devouring* you!'

She groaned. Was it that obvious? Her breasts rose and fell with her quickened breathing. 'You're exaggerating as usual,' she said hastily, casting a cool and disapproving glance at the arrogantly immune László. And although she tried to sound casual and offhand, she was maliciously thinking of embroidering his heart with stab stitches in hawser cable, nevertheless.

'You're keen, I can tell. Beware, darling. He does look deeply wicked—not the marrying sort at all!'

She laughed self-consciously at Mariann's teasing remark. 'For heaven's sake! I'm not husband-hunting!' she protested indignantly. 'Particularly in *that* direction. There's been enough of that lately! Nothing but husbands and fiancés——' She smiled at the countess, who'd come to take the spoiled dress. 'Don't let Mariann matchmake!' she appealed, trying to make a joke of it. 'I want to be an auntie dozens of times over before I even *think* of a relationship for myself.'

Mariann raised her eyes heavenwards. 'Leave me out of this hankering for babies! I'm not even married yet! I want to have fun and work for a while,' she cried, escaping hastily to the ballroom.

'Babies! How lovely!' sighed the countess. 'Girls or boys, I don't mind.' She took Sue's arm confidingly. 'I look forward to István's babies, you know. They'll all be Huszárs and the dynasty will live again. Every...' She faltered, then continued. 'Every direct descendant, male or female, is pledged to keep the family name. It's a tradition to ensure that we never die out.'

Suzanne nodded and stared at the portraits on the walls, hoping to convince the stranger that she wasn't at all concerned by his menacing stare. 'Odd, to be part of a dynasty,' she mused. 'I can understand the importance of keeping the line intact.'

'It's why I married a man I hated,' said the countess shakily, obviously remembering the bleak past. 'But I wish to God he'd stayed in Rostov where he came from!'

'Don't! It's all over now,' soothed Suzanne gently. 'Think of your grandchildren. They'll be running around in next to no time!' She beamed, happy to see the pleasure return to the woman's beautiful face. 'It must be ages since your son was born here,' she mused.

The countess went chalk white, the colour draining even from her lips. 'My—s-son?' she stumbled. 'There— there have been *no* babies born here! None!' she cried, almost hysterically.

It was obvious that the woman was struggling for every ounce of her iron self-control and Suzanne stared in astonishment at her reaction. 'István——' she began uncertainly.

'Born elsewhere. He was my love-child,' said the countess in agitation. 'I had to hide my pregnancy and his birth or be killed. The dynasty would be forfeit to the Russians! By the time my husband came back from the uprisings in Romania, István had been smuggled over the border by your mother and was safely in England.'

'How hard it must have been for you,' said Suzanne quietly, 'forced to marry one of the enemy who'd violated your country.'

'I had a duty,' rasped the countess, still pale as the creamy pearls at her throat. 'The inheritance before everything else, the thread of Hungary itself, running from generation to generation. Do you understand that?'

'I do,' she said huskily. Remembering that István's father had died crossing the border with István, her arm stole around the countess in sympathy. 'I think you're very brave,' she said softly, and decided not to pursue the truth of László's birth.

She had no wish to hurt the woman who had suffered so much—especially on this wonderfully happy day. Or...it had been happy, till *he'd* shown his face. Almost without intending to, she scanned the room, but he'd disappeared again, like a silent wraith. Only he was, unfortunately, all too real; flesh and blood and unnervingly vindictive. Whatever the cost, she must keep the two of them apart.

'What—what made you think my son was born here?' asked the countess, her voice harsh. 'What have people been saying?'

'A man——'

'*What man*?'

Oh, my God! thought Suzanne in horror, stunned by the hoarse outburst. Something was dreadfully wrong! For the countess's sake, she hastily hid her fears. 'Oh, dear!' she said lightly. 'I realise now, I used the wrong word! I've got it wrong. My Hungarian's let me down again! No wonder he looked as if I was talking a load of nonsense! Sorry to confuse you.'

She felt a hand on her arm and knew by the flip of her heart who it was. Slowly she turned her head to find László's unfathomable eyes on her.

'Hello, Suzanne,' he said quietly, his face strained as if he was holding back a tide of emotions. 'The countess,' he grated. 'Introduce me.'

She hesitated. The countess looked expectant, as though she had no idea who he was. Long, hard fingers crawled up her arm, pressing so deeply that she winced but she refused to show how he'd hurt her, choosing to pretend this was just another guest. And when she slanted her almond-shaped eyes to his, she saw that he had no idea he was hurting her at all, his whole being focused on the grey-haired woman in front of him.

'Countess Ana,' she rasped, 'this is László——'

'I'm a friend of Sue's,' he said soberly, kissing the offered hand which he held while he gazed deeply into the countess's eyes as if searching for something.

'How nice,' said Ana politely.

Then his body slumped and she realised he hadn't found it. Aware of him so acutely, she felt his disappointment, ridiculously ached for his carefully controlled despair. Because it was there, she knew. And however ruthless he might be, however amoral in his attitude towards eligible women, she couldn't fail to sympathise with his emotional pain.

'Countess, I am charmed,' he said quietly. There was an awkward pause. László seemed to be trying to get his emotions under control. Or, thought Suzanne, her heart hammering loudly, he was debating whether to reveal his secret. Her soft eyes pleaded with his. He smiled mockingly. 'I saw you both studying the family portraits,' he continued casually. 'Are those the Huszár seals?'

Her body shook with relief and was immediately steadied by his strong arm as though he was attuned to her body, too. Puzzled by his interest in the seals, Suzanne turned a little dazedly to look at the symbolic discs which were clasped proudly in the hands of each Huszár ancestor. And she wished his fingers weren't burning through her flimsy dress and massaging her ribs in time to the languid music.

'Oh, yes,' sighed the countess. 'They're medieval. *Were*,' she corrected harshly. 'My husband took them when——' She swallowed and licked dry lips, her expression bitter with hatred and Suzanne's expression became sympathetic. 'He took them to Russia. He knew what they meant to me but I never saw them again.'

László was breathing heavily. She hoped it wasn't because the melting of her body beneath his fingers was arousing him. 'I know your story, Countess,' he said softly, his voice deep with emotion. 'But I also know that your Russian husband is dead. And that a new phase of your life is about to start.'

He sounded surprisingly gentle and compassionate. But Suzanne could feel a tension in him that had turned every inch of his body to rock. Something to do with the Russian, she thought. With her heart in her mouth, she forced herself to think. Did he possess incriminating papers? Documents of sale, perhaps, issued by the Russians when they invaded Hungary? Maybe—oh, God! she groaned silently—maybe the estate wasn't legally István's any more!

Her eyes flashed to his. From his expression, he was struggling with conflicting thoughts. And then he opened his mouth to speak.

'Let's dance!' she said huskily, desperate to keep László from torturing the countess with lies—or, worse, the truth.

The tension streamed out of his body in a long sigh. 'Saved by the belle,' he muttered to himself sardonically.

The countess remembered the stained dress and headed for the housekeeper's quarters. Propelled by László's authoritative hand to the dance-floor, Suzanne turned a couple of times to watch the woman stumble once or twice and clutch at the panelling for support as though her legs were shaking uncontrollably. László's eyes followed hers. His hand increased its pressure and she realised he was simmering with suppressed anger.

László was a threat, without any doubt. But should she warn anyone—or would that destroy the occasion, and Tanya's future, as he'd suggested?

She took a deep, decisive breath. There was only one way to find out. Confront him and ask.

CHAPTER THREE

Suzanne felt torn. She needed to talk to László but feared being alone with him. A small thrill worked its way up from her toes to her head at the mere thought. And then she quivered as his hand slid from her slender spine, drifted to her waist and then gently pushed her around. Slowly her heavy lashes lifted.

'Come into my arms,' he said huskily.

He stood a couple of feet away, his hands held out to her. And inside her something was tumbling, making her sway with dizziness at the prospect. 'Asking you to dance was an excuse,' she croaked.

'I know,' he murmured. 'But one you'll fulfil before we go outside to talk and lay our cards on the table.'

'I don't want——' she croaked.

'But you do—and I insist.'

She looked down in confusion. As if stubbornly denying her lack of interest, her hands had reached out to touch his. Electric, she thought, astounded. In an instant, he'd swept her into his arms and they were moving over the floor as though they'd been bonded together, dipping, swaying supplely with the music, whirling faster and faster to the frenzy of the *csárdás*, the wild, foot-stamping tavern dance. But, instead of foot-stamping, László emphasised the beat by increased pressure on her back, thrusting her more surely into the hard male strength of his pelvis.

If she'd felt capable, she would have wrenched herself away. As it was, she felt so faint with the deep pulsating in her body and the smouldering in László's hypnotic eyes that she could only obey his every movement.

Inside her rose an excitement at the threatened release of years of tightly repressed and disciplined emotions. The frenzied music had intoxicated her; László's dazzling and mocking grin was encouraging her to tear loose from the restraints she'd put on herself.

Supple and pliant, she arched back to his command, thrilling to the sense of freedom he gave her by dancing with every fibre of his fluid body. It was primitive, pagan, and shocking.

And she loved it. Needed it. Feared and exulted in the discovery of a different woman entirely beneath her own skin. But was that bad, or was it good?

Suddenly she heard doors slam behind them, felt the cool air on her burning skin, opened her eyes with reluctance and discovered to her astonishment that they were outside on the candle-lit terrace, the scent of stocks filling the air.

But he didn't release her. For a moment she swayed in his arms in the drowsy silence, her senses uncomfortably alert to the wonderful hardness of his body, and she tried not to acknowledge the feminine thrill she felt on recognising that she had the power to excite him. This was dangerous, she thought, her heart leaping like that of a startled foal.

His finger tilted up her chin and she was forced to meet his eloquent eyes which held her as surely as though he'd chained her to him. 'You're a very surprising woman. There's more to you than I thought,' he murmured huskily.

'Remember that, when I puncture your ego and deflate your ludicrous sense of the dramatic!' she scathed defiantly.

He laughed softly and abandoned her abruptly, casually strolling down the steps to the drive. She would dearly have loved to turn her back on him and stalk back into the house but her legs wouldn't take her there—and she knew she had to face him out this time.

'Come on, Suzanne,' he taunted. 'You know we have to do this.'

She scowled. He was lounging against a centuries-old chestnut tree, the light from the avenues of tall, cast-iron braziers along the drive flickering like the flames of hell on his face. Summoning up all her nerve, she marched down the steps driven by pure adrenalin and stopped a few yards from him beside a brazier pole, the soft fabric of her silk chiffon dress fluttering in the warm summer breeze. Awash with sensation, she was intensely aware of his gaze, the set of his virile body, the scent of new-mown grass and the crackle of the red-gold flames above her head.

Without a word, he turned and walked towards the lake. And resentfully she followed, having no choice, and vowed to solve the mystery one way or another.

'You take a while to wind up,' he observed calmly, when they reached the edge of the whispering reeds.

She felt her blood boil. 'I'm not some clockwork toy——'

'You've been living like one, I understand.'

'Look, I'm not a malleable little dolly bird and I don't like being manipulated!' she ground out.

'Get used to it,' he murmured, smiling at her mutinous mouth. 'There's more to come. Sit on my jacket,' he ordered quietly, stripping it off and laying it on the ground.

Bolt upright beneath a lace canopy of beech trees, she sat as he'd directed while he remained standing, his legs straddled in an unconscious pose of domination.

'Talk,' she ordered curtly. 'You've been hinting that you have a proposition. Let's hear what it is.'

His eyes flickered with amusement. 'I was hoping to hear your plans first.'

She glanced up in surprise then looked away, unnerved by his hungry mouth. She was a fool, she thought in panic. His body oozed sexual vigour. 'OK. So you're stalling. I'm counting to ten and if you haven't given me an explanation of your odd behaviour then I'm going back,' she said in clipped tones.

'Don't be nervous,' he murmured. 'Unclench your hands and breathe or you'll go blue.' He laughed when she obeyed and then angrily jerked herself into rigidity again. 'You're looking for business contacts here, I understand.'

Suzanne's eyes widened and she looked at him from under her thick lashes. 'How did you know? Who's been talking about me?' she demanded in dismay.

'I have business connections with the textile people you've written to in Hungary.'

'Oh.' Her heart sank. That wasn't what she wanted to hear. He could make things difficult for her if he chose. 'Go on,' she muttered.

With a graceful movement, he came to sit close beside her, his hands loosely clasped over his knees. He was unusually still for a moment, but she had the impression that he could explode into life whenever he wished. It lent an air of waiting and expectancy to him and made her more on edge than ever. With the warm breeze came his now-familiar fragrance; a masculine tang, fresh and elusive, that made her want to lean closer. But she resisted. Of course. She wasn't *that* stupid.

'I can help you. That's what I meant about being an angel. Even I have to admit that I'm not likely to sprout wings,' he grinned lazily. 'I'm a financial angel, someone who loans money to people who need it.'

That wasn't what she'd been expecting to discuss. Warily her eyes slanted to see his expression, since the flat, unemotional tones had given nothing away. But all she saw in the half-light beneath the trees was a perfect, proud profile, the strong nose, the firm mouth and beautiful lines of his sculptured jaw. Then the dark, impenetrable eyes met hers and cast a spell on her of such animal intensity that she shrank into herself, afraid of his effortless ability to scatter her senses.

'Why would you want to help me?' she asked sullenly, hoping it wasn't the moneylenders' version of the casting couch.

'I admire and foster ambition.'

She gave him a scornful look. Unlikely. 'Then you must admire István!' she parried.

He laughed, the extraordinary fascination of his face and those compelling, limpid eyes that rested on her causing her triumph to turn to anxiety. 'I acknowledge his abilities,' he admitted, his voice low-pitched and throbbing. 'But at this moment it's you I'm interested in.'

She took a deep breath. It was the casting couch. 'Because you like to make young women grateful to you?' she asked coldly. 'You want a little bit of slavering adoration from some poor female you've helped on her way?'

'I'll ignore that,' he said drily. 'Let's establish a couple of points. You want to set up a mail-order business in your village, to bring much-needed employment there, to fulfil your dreams, perhaps...' His eyes narrowed. 'Perhaps to prove to your family that you're no longer a child——'

She started. No one knew that. How could he? 'I don't know what gives you that idea,' she said resentfully.

'It figures. You're the youngest in your family—I learnt that much from your brother when I talked to him earlier. I put two and two together. You see, I'm a student of human nature,' he answered softly. Her heart missed a beat as he wrestled his bow-tie loose and pushed it in his pocket. The thud in her body grew louder and more frantic while he undid the top two buttons of his startlingly white shirt and then it fell to a mere wild pounding when his hands came to rest on his knees again. 'What does that tell you?' he asked.

Secretly she lubricated her parched throat with a deep swallow. 'Your collar size was too small.'

His chuckle set up a small turbulence in her stomach. 'You'll have to do better than that if you're to be a businesswoman,' he scolded gently. 'You must learn to observe keenly, consider, understand. It should have told you that I can't stand restrictions, rules, convention. Remember that. Don't be surprised if I break a few. Did you make that dress?'

Exasperated, Suzanne repressed her irritation. She was beginning to get his methods sorted out. He liked to confuse, disorientate and distract, then sneak in with a few surprise remarks. 'Yes, and the two bridal gowns and the bridesmaids' dresses,' she answered as calmly as she could.

Her mind was ticking over. He knew the textile bosses.
If she had any sense, she'd impress him with her knowledge of the trade and press home some advantage. And
he was a money lender. She needed funds and he knew
that.

But... she'd have to be mad to get involved with him!
Her brow furrowed with the effort of understanding his
motives but was unable to see any connection between
those facts and the countess.

Defeated, she sighed and looked up to discover that
he was studying her dress with genuine admiration. His
astute gaze was taking in the seam detail, the drape of
the bodice and how she'd created a clean sweeping line
from breast to waist. And her whole body throbbed with
a flowing warmth that made her skin glow.

'Faultless,' he declared eventually. His guarded eyes
made her uncertain whether he was talking about her,
or the dress. 'I'd put my money on your success.'

'So would I, if I had any,' she replied coolly. 'But I'm
not intending to make clothes myself, only to work on
the designs and to set the standards for outworkers.'

'Precisely. And to do that, you will need to have high
standards yourself. You must know about design and
cutting and attention to detail. To handle suppliers at
such a distance—indeed, to succeed at all—you'll need
to work harder than any competitor. It's clear that you
drive yourself hard.'

'How?'

'From what you've achieved so far,' he said quietly.
'You've studied Hungarian, made plans for your future,
and held down a full-time job while producing outfits
for this wedding. It must have taken many hours to
produce that intricate beading on your sister's bridal
gown, for instance. And the ballgown that you're
wearing tonight—it...' A lushness claimed his sensual
mouth and she found herself unnervingly short of breath.
'There's hours of work in that. Successful hours.
It makes the most of your figure. Emphasises the
virginal.' The mouth became more wicked, more
greedily contemplative.

Virginal! There *was* a sexual intention behind all that flattery! Her anger flared. She'd been worrying all this time about some fictional danger he posed to Tanya and the others while he was merely lining her up for his bed!

'You spoilt your pitch,' she snapped. 'I thought you had something important to talk about!'

Haughtily half-rising, she was stopped by the quick touch of his hand on her thigh. Hot. Burning, in fact. Suddenly pliant, she sank to the soft, midnight-blue satin which lined his jacket, her senses disturbed by the brief but scalding caress.

'I have. More important than you could ever know. And for which I will gamble everything,' he said quietly, his supple body leaning towards her. And she focused her nervous eyes on the darkness of his deeply tanned throat where a deep pulse was beating, throbbing in the satin skin. 'I've always been a gambler,' he continued. 'But never more so than now. Gambling—successful gambling—requires finely tuned senses, considerable research, data bases and a great deal of intuition. It's highly creative. Those who turn it into a fine art, like me, are more aware of human failings and foibles than most. That's how I knew I could intrigue you enough to seek me out eventually and how I know you will agree to my request.'

'Oh, really?' she said in tones of disbelief.

'Yes. You don't like disorder, mysteries or untied threads. It was evident from your detailed and painstaking analyses in your letters to the textile bosses that you are a woman who is highly efficient and organised, hates muddle and likes to get everything nicely sewn up.'

Her sideways glance took in his smug smile. 'Can we get on with the sewing up, then?' she asked icily. 'I presume you have a purpose in mind. Surprise me with a demand that doesn't entail taking my clothes off.'

'It's a tempting thought, but not uppermost in my mind.' The dark eyes glimmered with sultry warmth. 'As a financial gambler, I take calculated risks on the money markets. When banks and venture capital syndicates won't back a proposal, I often will.' He looked deep into her eyes. 'I am better able than anyone I know at assessing a situation. It's a mixture of knowledge, research, intuition. In addition, I have no board, no colleagues to hold down my coat-tails. I am free to do whatever I like. That brings me to my interest in you.'

This was his proposition! Business! To her chagrin, she was almost annoyed that his interest seemed to be for commercial reasons and not her dazzling beauty! Her rueful grin slid across her mobile mouth. Where had that vanity come from? She gave him a shrewd look. 'You think I'm a good risk and——'

'I don't think you're any risk at all,' he replied, lifting a panel of her dress and apparently examining the shaping where it folded into the hip. Her skin contracted under the thin silk and flushed with heat. 'You can get hold of all the money you want, for a start. You have a rich brother-in-law now. Your sister Mariann will shortly be marrying Vigadó Gabór, one of the wealthiest men in Europe. Either could finance you——'

'Maybe they could, but I have no intention of asking for their help,' she said huskily. Clearing her throat of the annoying obstruction, she went on, 'I don't want anyone to think I'm using family money to smooth my path.'

'Good. Why?' he purred, sounding pleased.

She frowned. He had an annoying ability of caressing her with his voice. It was highly distracting. With difficulty, she brought her mind back to his question.

'What achievement would there be in that? The rest of my family had no help. Tanya has shown she can handle a business of her own; Mariann climbed to the post of editor because of her own talent—even before she met Vigadó.'

'You aren't exactly at the bottom of the ladder,' he murmured.

'No, I've done well,' she acknowledged without false modesty. 'Since you've seen my details, you'll know that I was a member of a highly regarded team in the costume department of the Glyndebourne opera company.' Taken up with the thing that mattered deeply to her, she leaned forward eagerly. 'But you see, however exciting it is, creating stunning costumes from an almost unlimited budget isn't the same as showing total faith in your independence and ability by striking out on your own. You're right,' she said fervently, her eyes ablaze with passion. 'I do have an all-consuming ambition to run my own company—and to lose the tag of being the "baby" of the family!'

'I see no baby,' he said gravely. 'And I do know what you're talking about. Being the last in a large family can be frustrating.' He smiled faintly, his expression far-away. 'The youngest child,' he mused, almost to himself, 'is doomed to be the last in the line for everything.'

Sweet, gentle curves appeared on the hard male mouth. Suzanne felt a lurch in her heart.

'That's true! You've hit the nail on the head!' she cried a little shakily. At last someone understood—though she would have preferred it to be anyone but the all-knowing László! 'I suppose you're the youngest in a large family too,' she said slowly.

'No.' He smiled at her baffled expression. 'Look, just accept that I sympathise with your aims and that I know you want to achieve success on your own. Do you have a backer?'

She shook her head in regret, knowing what was coming. 'No. It's too early for the English banks to risk anything. I have to get some promises from the textile companies first——'

'You have now. I will help you to achieve your ambition,' he said softly.

She'd been half expecting that offer, but was still startled. And reluctantly she shook her head. How easy it would be to thank him and wait for his cheque! But she had the distinct feeling that his help would have strings—and there was still the matter of the danger he might pose to the countess.

'No, thanks. I'd rather look elsewhere,' she said firmly. 'If you think I'm no risk at all then so will others, eventually.'

'Then I think I'd better tell you that you'll get no-where in Hungary without me.'

Alerted by the malicious tone, her head jerked up. 'Is that a threat?' she asked in horror.

'A promise,' he amended and the dark eyes were hard with a forbidding hostility.

'You bastard!' she cried, flushing with angry astonishment.

'No. Not by any means,' he drawled. 'Unlike your brother-in-law István.'

Eyes glittering with fiery lights, she jumped up. But he caught her hand, jerking her off-balance and easily pulled her to the ground again, her body slipping on the satin lining of his jacket so that she ended up on her back. And this time he hovered above her like a lover about to claim his first kiss.

'Get away from me or I'll scream!' she hissed furiously, bewildered that she felt both excited and frightened.

He smiled faintly and traced the line of her collarbone while she remained struck dumb with fear, her eyes huge dark saucers in her pale face. 'And then István will come running, and Tanya, and perhaps the Countess Ana Huszár.' His hand paused on her shoulder, gripping it tightly. 'And I will tell them who I am and their lives will be shattered. You can't do that to them,' he murmured with satin softness.

Dark, silken strands of hair had tumbled over her face. From beneath her lashes, she gazed at him in horror, acutely aware of the fierce waves of male desire pouring from his tense body. But that was nothing compared with his malevolent determination to wreak some unnamed havoc in the life of the Huszár family.

'How will they be shattered? *Who are you*?' she rasped.

A finger flicked back the long strands of her inky hair. 'My family name on my mother's side,' he said, a malicious pleasure in his eyes, 'is Huszár.'

'Hu . . . szár!'

Suzanne's intake of breath rasped painfully in her throat as she stared up at him uncomprehendingly. Then, desperate to free herself, she thrust out her hands in an almost hysterical gesture. To her dismay, he'd seen her intention with those damnable all-seeing eyes and had caught her wrists in a tight lock, his lean fingers unrelenting as she grappled with him in an undignified struggle.

'Let me go!' she seethed, half-sobbing. 'How *dare* you treat me like this?'

'Because I obviously have a very powerful hold over you, physical and mental,' he answered with infuriating mildness. 'And can do almost anything I like. Now there's a thought.'

She stopped struggling and just scowled. Already she'd noticed that her furious writhing had lit a light in his dark eyes that was pure, naked lust. 'You don't, you can't,' she said nervously. 'Your claim is absolute nonsense! The countess and István are all that's left of the family. That's why he's so precious to her——'

'He's precious to her because he's the son of her lover and until a few years ago she hadn't seen him since he was born,' growled László savagely, anguish marking every inch of his face. 'Every time she looks at him, she remembers the man she fell in love with when she was thirty years old. And she loved with all the pent-up passion of a woman who'd lived half a lifetime without knowing the meaning of true love. No wonder the little bastard is precious!' he snarled under his breath.

At the loathing in his words, her eyes widened in alarm. It would have been obvious to anyone that he wasn't lying, or joking, or making exaggerated claims. He hated the countess and István to the very roots of his being. And that meant... She felt herself panicking. Carefully, with the utmost effort, she steadied her mind. Losing her wits wouldn't help. She had to keep calm and in control if she was to help Tanya.

'As you say, that's natural,' she said huskily, relieved that the pressure on her wrists was easing. 'The countess had been unhappily married for years.'

'Exactly! She was *married*!'

The harsh, brutally bitten-off words told her what he thought of adultery. 'I know,' she said quietly, trying to speak for the absent countess. 'I agree. It was wrong. But how can you help it when a devastating love sweeps you off your feet——?'

'If you're married, you don't make yourself available,' he snarled, his teeth white and feral beneath the stretched lips. 'Marriage is forever. You must have the courage and the strength of will to walk away from any temptation——'

'It's never that easy,' she argued, finding herself defending something she didn't personally agree with. But she couldn't side with László and his unusually fierce belief in fidelity. 'In this case, the countess hated and despised her husband because he was a Russian——'

'She married him!' he roared, his voice shaking with anger. 'It was her decision to do that and she wilfully, deliberately set out to capture him! If you make a conscious and premeditated choice, you must pay the price of that choice.' László's face was dark with anger, the mask of control slipping at last. 'She chose to use Nikolai Romanov for the benefits that associating with a member of the Politburo would bring——'

'But he'd requisitioned her house and lands and was threatening to destroy everything she loved!' wailed Suzanne.

'It was a time of war!'

'Invasion,' she corrected hotly, 'and the countess had little choice at all! Was she to see the place wrecked? The houses laid to waste, the villagers who'd served her family for centuries turned into refugees or worse? Dozens of people relied on her. It was in her power to save a whole village, a way of life—and she would have been less of a woman if she'd simply put her own feelings first!'

At that, he was still, their breathing the only movement, the only sound between them. And the mask had returned to smooth over his face in the same way that the melting ice on the sculpted huszar had blurred its features. Supplely graceful, he regained his feet and looked down at her. She felt her heart chill at his frozen, implacable silence and raised her slim body, the better to defy him.

'You are so very beautiful,' he purred thoughtfully.

Somehow she controlled her impulse to hit him. 'That's not true!' she stormed. 'Stick to the point! What are you up to?' she asked bluntly, her chin set in stubborn anger. 'And what precisely are you claiming is your relationship with István?'

He considered for a long moment and she felt her skin prickling with nerves. Then he took a deep breath and told her, slowly, his voice ringing with emotion. 'You're the first ever to hear this. I hope you're conscious of the honour,' he mocked. But there was bitterness streaking across his glittering eyes and she cringed, waiting for the blow. 'I'm István's half-brother. The son of Nikolai Romanov and the countess. The rightful heir to the Huszár estates and entire fortune.'

There was a deathly silence and then she scrambled up, stumbled, recovered herself with a tremendous effort. Not caring that she was only inches away from his threatening body, she stood there gathering her senses for a moment while he looked on in brutal indifference to her distress.

'You—can't be!' she said jerkily. 'She—she had no other child——'

'Who said?' he grated.

'She did!' Gleaming strands of her hair dipped over one eye and she tossed them back irritably, just catching the remains of a wince that had tightened the skin across his high cheekbones. Her stomach lurched. That had hurt him. The implication wasn't lost on her but she persisted in denying his claim because she had to, for everyone's sake. 'The countess said that no baby had been born in the house!' she challenged.

His expressive mouth was grimly clamped over clenched teeth and he drew in a vast breath and released it as if to release some of the fury that was making his body quiver.

'Of course she'd deny that!' he muttered. 'She's been trying to blot me out of her life ever since I was born. But István is the bastard. I am legitimate. I am also—as you will have noticed—older than him. Ten years, to be exact.'

'You can't be a Huszár!' she moaned stubbornly.

'Oh, I am. Sometimes I wish to God I were not,' he growled. 'It's a legacy I'd prefer not to have inherited. I'm known to the world as László Lázár. In my home town in Russia, I'm regarded as a Romanov. Here,' he set his jaw belligerently, 'like it or not, I am a Huszár. And I have the whip hand, Suzanne. You're standing on my land. You've been dancing in my castle, sleeping in my bed. In fact, the whole damn lot of you are trespassing and I could have you all ejected within hours.'

'Oh, my God! You wouldn't...' Her voice trailed away as the full meaning of his revelation penetrated her frozen brain. If it was true... She gulped, terror gripping her mind as she saw the destruction of Tanya's happiness, the anguish on István's face...

'If you want incontrovertible proof, you can take a look at my birth certificate, since you read Russian. I brought it along specially for you, knowing you'd be here.'

It was all planned, she thought dizzily. Everything he'd done and said had been carefully orchestrated before he'd even set foot on István's land. *László's* land! she corrected miserably. 'Where is it?' she whispered. 'I have to see it.'

Mocking her with his ruthless eyes, he lifted a slender wallet from his breast pocket and flicked through it, finding what he wanted. She scanned the document he handed to her several times before she could take it in.

'A forgery!' she declared shakily.

'We can get it verified—if you dare,' he said, serenely assured. 'Of course, you'll recognise these. The family seals.' And to her horror, they were in his hand; plaster duplicates of the ones in the Huszár portraits.

'You've stolen them!' she accused in horror, thinking how he must have been smirking inside when they'd discussed them, knowing they were in his pocket all the time. Her eyes flashed with temper. 'They belong to——'

'Me!' he curtly reminded her, and she bit her lip with frustration. 'I came by them honestly. My father placed them in my possession when he took me back to his home in Rostov. They were mine, after all, weren't they?'

Suzanne went deathly pale. There was no doubt in her mind any more. He knew too much. She remembered her conversation with the countess, the mention of Rostov and the woman's apparently irrational terror at the mention of a baby being born in the castle. She felt her body drain of all life.

'Why would your father take you away if you were the heir?' she whispered faintly.

Crackling hostility poured from his narrowed eyes, the thin line of his mouth stretched like a snarl over his teeth. 'Security. The countess vowed that a Russian would never inherit Huszár land,' he growled and his voice began to shake. 'Bitch of a mother that she was!' he breathed hoarsely.

'No!' cried Suzanne, profoundly upset. Sons didn't hate their mothers! Her hand flew to her mouth, the fingers fluttering in shock. What had he felt, she wondered, greeting his own mother like a stranger? 'Oh, God!' she whispered, appalled by what was happening. 'No woman hates her son!'

'She did,' he muttered. 'I was the enemy——'

'No! A baby? Her baby?' breathed Suzanne.

László's beautiful, sensual mouth was drawn taut across his teeth in a frighteningly feral snarl. 'A baby!' he growled. 'Defenceless, blameless, but half Russian. In her eyes I represented the enemy. You don't know what it was like in those times, the hatred that pervaded the country,' he muttered. 'I was born shortly after the Hungarian uprising—and its subsequent crushing by Russian tanks which rolled over the border and put the fear of God into every national. Hungary was a hotbed of political unrest. Men disappeared, never to be seen again. Who'd wonder about a Russian's baby?'

'No, László!' she wailed. 'The countess isn't like that, she loves children——'

'But not me,' he grated. 'I'd robbed her of the one thing she wanted: a pure Hungarian heir. Father told me that she'd expected the war to end after a few years, eventually releasing her to marry the man of her choice. But she was horrified to find herself pregnant, appalled when Hungary remained under the Russian yoke. My father knew how she felt. He was away frequently and the countess wasn't to be trusted with me——'

'She was your mother!' cried Suzanne passionately. 'She'd instinctively protect you——'

'Like hell!' he spat. 'She hated me—and would have killed me, given half a chance!'

'I don't believe it,' she retorted miserably, stubbornly shutting her mind to the terrible knowledge that it might just be true. He was poisoning her mind. The countess was compassionate. She would have loved her little baby, whoever the father might have been. She passed a fretful hand over her forehead. Above the distant strains of a Strauss waltz came the molten notes of the nightingale again, mocking her with its joy. A groan shuddered through her. There would be no joy in the family when László confronted them all. He'd chosen the happiest day... Her head snapped up. 'Why come here now?' she demanded fiercely. 'Why wait all this time?'

'Because of the restrictions of living in a Soviet world,' he said curtly. 'Indifference, too. I wasn't interested in some scrap of Hungarian dirt, a few lumps of stone and a village full of people who'd gladly strangle me in my bed.'

'Your mother——' she began.

He scowled. 'I was taught to loathe and despise everything Hungarian—especially her.'

'That's cruel,' moaned Suzanne unhappily.

'Life's cruel!' he snapped. 'Particularly when my father died in the service of my country, and with him vanished any influence we had: the permissions for travel, the perks that went with his job.'

Suzanne frowned, feeling the stirrings of sympathy. He'd been brought up to hate his mother and that was terrible. She studied his dark face surreptitiously. He looked haggard with anguish, driven by a lifelong revenge. And her family was in his path. Only she could do something to divert him, and the burden was crushing her already.

CHAPTER FOUR

SOMEHOW she had to persuade László that there was merit in conciliation: that he'd gain more by showing love to his mother and binding himself to the family. But... She frowned. That would mean he'd take over the estate and it would pass from István's capable hands. And her heart wanted Tanya and her brother-in-law to live here and bring up their children. This outsider had no place here, no place at all!

Heart and mind were in opposition for once. She despaired of reconciling them. All she could do for now was to get him to talk, because she still didn't know quite what he had in mind and she needed to be sure of his goal before she stuck herself in front of it.

'When your father died,' she said gently, 'were you left alone?'

'No. I still had my grandparents.' László turned his head to where a pheasant had croaked, a terrible emptiness in his glittering eyes, and inexplicably she wanted to offer some gesture of comfort because his hurt was so deep. He threw his strong head back, the moonlight turning his throat to a pillar of silvered skin. 'I fell foul of the Soviet régime as a teenager,' he said softly, 'and fled to America. I didn't come here, because I didn't want to. I was busy making my fortune. I had something to prove to myself... that I had some value.'

She bit her lip. He'd felt rejected by his mother. It was so sad. 'May I see the seals?' she asked, hoping to find a way of returning them.

'They're genuine,' he told her curtly. 'Look: the two-headed eagle, the flowers and the sheaf of corn.'

'They belong here,' she said slowly.

'As I do,' he pointed out coldly.

'But you don't, do you?' she said earnestly, her small face pinched and anxious. 'You've made a life elsewhere—successfully, by the way you dress and behave——'

'However successful I may be, it signifies nothing when a part of my life has been erased. Perhaps you should ask the countess about the baby who was born in the castle, thirty-seven years ago——'

'Her heart might not stand the shock!' cried Suzanne, wide-eyed.

'I agree—you see,' he said with malevolent relish, 'she was told that I was dead. My father wanted to protect me from any chance that, as his wife, she might gain access to me in Rostov.' His voice hardened. 'She didn't care. She loathed the sight of me from birth and was only too glad for her beloved István to take the title. But there are people in the village who would remember the existence of a child who screamed night and day because he was never picked up, never loved,' he said huskily.

She swayed, as he must have known she would because his arm was already there around her waist. And she felt her limp body being drawn to lie against him, her breasts pressing firmly against his shirt front, her cheek lying on his heart. Which pounded with a violence that startled her till she realised hers was faster, more erratic still.

He said nothing. Crushed against his powerful body, her thoughts whirled in chaotic disarray. 'My sister has only just found happiness,' she said in a small voice, 'and her world is about to be cracked apart!'

'Perhaps. That depends on you. It's ironic that it's you, the youngest member of your family, who holds their future in her hands,' muttered László, softly in her ear. 'You can—if you choose—prevent this information becoming common knowledge.'

'*What*? How?' she gasped, arching back sharply to search his watchful eyes.

'By co-operating with me.'

She stiffened, realising that László's hand was lightly caressing her spine and her treacherous body was enjoying the sensation. A strange, warm feeling was pervading every fibre, every muscle, her flesh melting. In her ear she could hear the rasp of his breath, quickening with every languid movement of his hand. Now she was sure of his purpose. Sexual blackmail. Her befuddled mind wouldn't tell her why—why her.

She groaned inwardly, sensing with her newly attuned antennae his barely contained passions. He was not the kind of man who'd rein in his sexual urges. He was quite ruthless and determined to get his own way. If he wanted her, he'd take her.

Her head tipped back and she opened her mouth to protest. But he muttered under his breath and fastened his avid eyes hungrily on her parted lips.

A small shudder caused her body to slide against his. With a soft, guttural sound he let one hand enjoy the curve of her waist and hip, then crawl to her thigh while she fought for speech, dizzy and alarmed at the quick inflammation of his passion.

'This is a bonus I hadn't planned on. I want you, I actually want you!' growled László in a rough undertone.

'*No!*' she cried, appalled. His arms were like a vice suddenly, crushing her hard against him till she felt the heat of him burn into the whole length of her body and focus in one, throbbing place.

'It must be apparent. At such close quarters I can hardly hide the evidence,' he said sardonically. 'I must admit, it will make what I have in mind a little easier. More pleasant.'

Deliberately he gyrated his pelvis in a slow, sensuous movement against hers. It should have been coarse, vulgar, insulting. Instead, she found herself deeply affected by his need, shockingly eager for him to move against her again and relieve the incomprehensible urge for the pressure of his body.

Stunned, humiliated by the hot wave of desire that flooded through her at the discovery of his sexual craving, she whimpered in despair and rage.

'You're——' She had to fight to find her voice, to rid herself of the terrible hoarseness in her throat. 'You're behaving like an animal! You've inherited the brutality of your father and his invading troops!' she blurted out wildly, desperate for anything, *anything* to free her.

She felt the jerk of his body as the words punched into him like a physical blow and knew she'd made a dreadful mistake even before he pushed her back till her spine nearly cracked.

'You *bitch*!' he spat.

Petrified, she was caught like a rabbit by his triumphant and merciless stare, and slowly he bent his head to kiss her, ignoring her desperately whispered pleas for mercy.

The impact on her mouth bent her further still and they fell to the ground. Hard as the ground itself, his body lay on hers, his mouth greedily exploring, and she was utterly helpless beneath his weight. With nerves clutching like claws at her stomach, she fought when and where she could, avoiding his mouth, turning her head this way and that, grappling with his hands, arms; protecting herself from him... and as the kiss deepened, became less of an assault and more of a velvet embrace, she began to protect herself from the terrible urge she had to prolong the exhilarating possession of her bruised mouth.

It was like the fires of hell burning inside her. Swimming in deep water. Battling through a tornado. Nothing had prepared her for the kiss of a man who knew where, how to use his mouth and tongue and teeth... She groaned, making small whimpering sounds in her throat. His lips softened and she wanted him to lie there with her for ever, teaching her passion, slaking her thirst for his mouth.

Somewhere far back in her mind she found her conscience. It was grieving that she was so eager to respond to him. And miserably she knew that he was all animal and she must deny herself this hungry male tiger. She shuddered, feeling earthy, hungry, voracious...

There came the sound of tearing material where she'd jerked herself free, leaving some of the ethereal silk chiffon beneath his hip. But she could leap to her feet and run! Run from her shocking feelings, the blaze of delight his pagan assault had created inside her. Run from the truth. Her pagan self, her wantonness.

'Oh no!' she moaned. Her feet had stumbled, weakened by a warm yielding of her limbs and he'd caught her flying hair. 'Owww!' she yelled.

'Keep still, then. I've not finished with you yet!' László grimly turned her around. The blind fury in his face frightened her into a numbed silence. Despite the deceptively smooth exterior lay a man stripped bare of all his carefully acquired civilised veneer and who burned with a barely-controlled savage hunger.

'I will not be mauled about!' she raged hysterically as he slid his hand up her neck.

'For a woman facing possible rape, you show admirable reserves of courage,' he grated, his eyes gleaming feverishly. The hand lay circling her throat, his thumb on her wild pulse. 'And a particularly vicious tongue,' he mused. 'I'm tempted to punish you——'

'By humiliating me?' she retorted indignantly. Rape, she was thinking, her heart in her mouth. Rape! 'Let me *go*!'

'Not yet,' he muttered, his hot breath whispering over her mouth, making it quiver expectantly. 'And I'd advise you not to test my temper. I'll have no compunction in using whatever means necessary to get what I want.' He glowered from beneath the black line of his brows. 'I warn you: never, ever, speak ill of my father again. Or I swear that I will lay you out beneath me and really teach you what the ultimate humiliation is for a woman such as you.' He drew in a long, angry breath. 'Just remember,' he snarled. 'I will not have his memory sullied by anyone! *Anyone*! Do you hear?'

She closed her eyes in utter dismay. There was no doubt that he was Nikolai's son. Her insult had unleashed an explosive defence. The cruelly tightening hand had relaxed and was lightly resting on her shoulder.

Warily, she shot him a quick, assessing look, sensing that his anger had run its course.

'I'm sorry,' she said, ashen-faced. 'I'm ashamed of myself for insulting your father. It wasn't Christian. But I was...' She paused, not wanting him to know that she'd been petrified.

'Scared?' he suggested.

'Angry,' she corrected tightly, furious that her feelings had been so transparent. 'But we're quits. I was rude, you took your revenge. That's not the issue any more; there's something far more important for us to discuss.' Her voice shook at the enormity of the situation.

'My inheritance,' he said softly.

'Yes.' She gulped and licked her dry lips, the words sticking in her throat. Her huge eyes lifted pleadingly to his. 'I want to ask you a favour,' she croaked.

'I know.'

She bit back her irritation. If nothing else, László was teaching her to consider her words before she spoke. 'I know you want me to co-operate with you and that I've made it clear that I'm not sharing my body with anyone, let alone you,' she said huskily. 'But I have to ask you...' Miserable at the thought of what he could do to Tanya, she threw back her head and fixed him with wet-fringed eyes, her spiky lashes fluttering as she attempted not to give way completely and burst into tears. 'Please!' she begged in a low undertone. 'If you have any pity at all, give István and Tanya this one day, this lovely, perfect day, to remember!'

'I'm a businessman,' he said cynically. 'I don't have room for pity.' His expression became mocking at the groan that escaped from her weakly parted lips. 'I'm open to bargaining, though,' he taunted, playing her like a fish on a line.

Her body felt like a leaden weight. No wonder she was drowning in the darkness. 'I'd rather bargain with the devil!' she said hoarsely.

'I think you'll find me marginally less unpleasant to deal with,' he drawled sarcastically. 'And I am, at least, giving you a choice——'

'I refuse to make any arrangement with you!' she said harshly.

'You're not interested in sleeping with me?' he enquired in a mocking tone.

Suzanne gaped at him. It was as though he was wondering if she wanted to fit double-glazing. She couldn't contain herself any longer. 'You're totally immoral!' she seethed. 'If you want me to make myself sexually available to you, and in exchange you'll let Tanya have a few days of ignorance——'

'Would you agree to those terms?' he murmured.

She felt nauseous. Forgive me, Tanya, she thought, knowing her sister would understand. 'No,' she replied hoarsely.

'I see. Then we must find a compromise between my needs and yours somehow. Let me tell you what I want—what I really want,' he said, his face impassive. 'Or at least, the first part——'

'All, tell me all of it!' she demanded in agitation.

'Patience is a game I've learnt over the years,' he drawled. 'It would do you no harm to learn it too. You see, Suzanne, I only put some of my cards on the table at any one time. The rest I keep close to my chest. Be content with that for the moment. I will agree to drop all claim to the estate and the title. In exchange, I will finance you.'

'*What*?' she gasped. 'Why?'

'There has to be something in it for you, or you won't co-operate, will you? I can smooth your path when you arrange your contacts in the textile co-operatives,' he said calmly while her eyes widened in astonishment. 'I'm prepared to be with you every step of the way.'

There was no logic to that. Suzanne passed a trembling hand over her forehead and fixed him with a bewildered stare. She gave a short, mirthless laugh of disbelief. 'That's crazy! You'd be doing me a favour!'

'Then we'll both be satisfied, won't we?' he said drily. 'You're wondering why I should do this, of course—what's in it for me. It's simple. I want you to be a thorn in István's side—and Vigadó's.' He smiled bitterly. 'And incidentally to annoy the countess.'

'For what reason?' she asked warily.

'We've all been business rivals for years. There's a deal I want to make,' he answered abruptly.

'A deal.' Her solemn eyes scanned his. It would have to be something very big for him to trade his inheritance for it, and some inner caution made her reluctant to believe him.

'It's important to me,' he said softly. 'Worth any sacrifice.'

Not the chance to turn down the ultimate pleasure of taking over the Huszár dynasty though, she thought. And vowed to keep working on him till he gave himself away. 'If you're a business rival, why didn't anyone recognise you?' she asked suspiciously.

'I keep a very low profile,' he replied without hesitation. 'I might be a well-known name on the international scene, but very few people know me by sight. I shun publicity and delegate all public appearances to my senior executives. Apart from giving me a welcome anonymity, it's paid me handsomely to remain unidentifiable. I can move freely in financial markets and wander into rival companies to observe their operations.' The black eyes flashed, revealing the volcanic anger again. 'Vigadó in particular would be appalled to know that you and I were partners. It would give me a lever so I could scotch his plans to humiliate me. And that would amuse me vastly.'

She had the distinct feeling that he wasn't telling her the whole truth and if Vigadó despised László too, then she felt even more wary of linking herself with him, for whatever reason. 'I don't like your sense of humour,' she muttered. 'The idea of me, deliberately hurting István and——'

'Better for your brother-in-law to feel betrayed by you,' interrupted László sardonically, 'than the loss of his title and lands. Think, Suzanne. Consider the distress the countess would suffer, should she ever discover that her hated first-born is not dead as she thought, but alive and kicking and returning to the fold with vengeance in his heart and claims in his hands to the Huszár estates.'

It would break the countess, she thought in alarm. Her lands would go to the son of the husband she'd loathed and despised. While her beloved István—who'd only recently returned to her after a lifetime's separation—would be disinherited. The whole thing was appalling.

'What a brute you are!' she said coldly.

'Someone must have made me that way,' he said with quiet reproof and she heaved a ragged sigh of despair.

'When did the countess last see you...before today?'

'I was barely a year old when I left here,' he answered curtly. 'But I gather she never set eyes on me, never held me in her arms, never enquired after my health.'

She felt a hopelessness fill her heart and something akin to sympathy for him. And wondered with more than a little pity what it must be like never to know your mother—and to be aware of her contempt and hatred for your father. She lifted her head and groaned aloud. The unhappy marriage between the countess and Nikolai Romanov had touched many lives and caused a great deal of misery. The circumstances of István's birth had been problematic enough, but this...

'She never recognised you,' she said, her expression tragic.

'Show me no pity,' he said expressionlessly. 'She rejected me. I had to get used to that——'

'But you didn't.'

He started, his face briefly vulnerable with sorrow. 'Cut the sympathy. I don't want it.'

'You must have had a terrible childhood!' she exclaimed sadly, her voice shaking a little.

'On the contrary,' he snapped. 'I had a great deal of love and care from my grandparents.'

'But...it—it must have been painful, entering this house,' she ventured huskily.

'Farcical.'

She chewed her lip. He was very bitter. Into her mind came the image of a man wandering around a castle that should have been his home, coldly watching a family celebration over which he might have presided. What had he made of the love and affection between them all? She gave an involuntary shiver as she studied his neutral face. It wasn't his fault, not any of it. He did have a legal right to the land. That left her in an awkward situation.

'This land, the castle... it all belongs to you,' she said painfully. 'We ought to find a way to tell the countess. It should be yours.'

László's dark eyebrow winged up in surprise. 'Surely you're not turning my proposition down?'

'I'm trying to do what's *right*!' she wailed miserably. 'Looking at this from a legal, logical point of view, you should be the count. What right have I—or any of us— to stand in your way?'

'My God!' he marvelled. 'A woman with principles! That's not what I'd bargained for!' He seemed confounded for a moment, as though she'd turned his plans inside out, and then his mouth quirked wryly and he said, 'Perhaps I'd better tell you what I'd do if I took over the estate. You might decide to change your noble little mind. Of course, it goes without saying that I'd throw the countess out on her ear after her son and your sister. Then I'd sack everyone—including your brother John and his new bride—and employ Russians to look after me. I'd refuse permission for any villager to work the land so that the village would fall into disuse——'

'But that's monstrous! Why on earth would you destroy everything you'd acquired?' she gasped.

'Because I don't want it—I have no need for any of it—and it would give me pleasure to know that it had been ruined,' he said calmly. 'I'd let the house and gardens fall into decay, too. A fitting revenge. The Huszár dynasty would die out as if it had never existed. Yes... I like the idea.'

'You evil brute!' she seethed.

'Ruthless,' he agreed harshly. 'I'm not playing for buttons, Suzanne. Make no mistake about it: this deal I'm bargaining for is the most crucial one of my life and if I don't make it, if you don't fall in with my plans, then I'll be going to hell and you can bet your sweet life that I'm making sure I take my enemies with me. Excuse me. I think I'll go to István and tell him who I am.'

Grimly László began to walk towards the softly lit castle.

'No! Wait!' she cried hoarsely, reeling from his vehemence. He stopped, but didn't return. For a moment she stared rebelliously at his broad, arrogant back and the imperious set of his head and then let out a resigned groan and went to him. She felt completely manipulated, and it irked her to be losing control of the threads of her life.

He had a legal right to the lands and she ought to accept that. But there was a moral right involved: the well-being of her family. Which took precedence? Perhaps she should protect her family and the future of Kastély Huszár, rather than go strictly by the book. She just didn't know what to do. And she desperately needed time to think.

'Don't speak to him yet. You must understand this has been a shock. Give me a couple of days to consider——' she began.

Frowning, he checked his watch. 'No. I'll have your decision now. István will leave for his honeymoon soon. Before he does, I want to give him a wedding gift he'll never forget. Either we confront him with the news that you're joining forces with the man he thinks is a crook and a liar, or we tell him that he has been disinherited. Time's running out, Suzanne. Decide.'

She went white. 'Whatever happens, you mean to wreck his wedding-day——'

László grabbed her arms roughly. 'You fool!' he scorned. 'Of course! Do you think I intended to keep quiet about our collaboration?' He smiled cynically. 'That's a good word: collaboration. It's a habit of this family to co-operate with the enemy when faced with trouble, isn't it?'

'You evil-minded sadist!' Her head jerked up. 'I can't do it!' she grated. This was a nightmare. It couldn't be happening. She needed to stall, to think of a way out,

to wake up and find she'd fallen asleep on a ballroom
chair. 'Let me have more time,' she wheedled. And made
her mouth form into a travesty of a smile. 'I never make
decisions lightly. I always think things through with great
care, weighing up the pros and the cons——'

'So I understand,' he growled. 'The careful type.
That's why I'm giving you no time at all. Decide now,
or I take the matter into my own hands.'

'I love my family,' she said, her voice trembling with
emotion. 'If you ever loved anyone, you'll know what
this would do to them and to me. Think of what you
felt for your own father——' She gasped, her head
snapped back as he shook her in temper and she felt the
harsh rasp of his laboured breath on her softly protesting lips.

'Don't try to soften me with talk of loving families!
Yes or no?' he snarled.

She shut her eyes again to his malevolent face, tried
to block out her inevitable betrayal of the people she
loved by allying herself with István's business rival. But
in her heart of hearts she knew that it was a lesser evil.
It was the price—a relatively small one—she had to pay
for the sake of saving István's future and Tanya's; for
the long-suffering countess's peace of mind and even for
the sake of the castle, the villagers and the estate itself.

'Yes,' she whispered, her body as stiff as buckram.
Her eyes blazed into his. 'I'll do it!' she muttered resentfully, 'but unwillingly. And I want to make it absolutely clear that I hold you in utter contempt for
making me a party to your vile revenge!'

His breath exhaled in a gravelly rasp, the taut muscles
relaxing as though he didn't care what she thought of
his character at all. It was fine for him, she thought miserably. He had what he wanted: a chance to crow over
István's discomfiture. The man was petty. Unless . . . she
remembered that this was the first stage of his revenge.
He had more cards to play and she dreaded to know
what they might be.

Her mind reeled with thoughts of what would happen, how everyone would take the news that she'd defected to one of István's despised enemies.

Desperate to know exactly why he was rejecting a life of luxury and power, she knew she dared not ask. He might reconsider and kick the countess and István—and Tanya, John and Lisa!—off the estate by producing his birth certificate and the family seals.

'Oh, God!' she groaned aloud.

'Come,' he ordered, quite unmoved by her distress. 'We'll announce our arrangement.'

'I—I——' She shrank back, her eyes huge dark pools in the paleness of her face. Scorn swept across his dark eyes, making her head lift in pride. 'All right,' she breathed huskily. 'Let's get it over with.'

'So you're brave, too,' he murmured.

That wasn't worthy of comment. Besides, her throat was closing in misery and tears were forming behind her lowered lashes. Walking like an automaton beside the hated László, she felt herself tremble as they approached the castle.

Her steps became slower, more faltering. László put his arm around her waist to urge her on. Perhaps she should have shrugged him off, but she needed that support, or else she would have crumpled to the ground.

Never in her life had she acted deviously or told an intentional out-and-out lie. Shame filled her whole body, despite the logic that kept telling her it was for the best. And it was ironic that she'd always lived by logic, had always considered all the angles and followed whichever route seemed most sensible.

This time she felt different about taking the most prudent course. This time there were other factors involved: her love for her family, her self-respect and her intense dislike of the man who was giving her financial aid. It was the first occasion that her emotions had unwillingly been dragged into a decision she was making, and the more she thought about the next few minutes the more uncertain she became about how she'd handle it.

'Stop a minute,' she croaked, when they'd reached the top of the steps and stood outside the baronial door. 'Don't rush me... I need *time*——'

'I'll do the talking. You don't have to say a word,' he murmured, holding her steady in his arms.

To her astonishment, his mouth descended ruthlessly on hers, firing her with... anger? life? Oh, God! she thought weakly as the kiss gentled with an unwanted sweetness and tore into her body, I'm muddled! What's he doing to me?

The kiss deepened and it was as if she began to unfurl like the petals of a flower. After a moment she found herself clinging to him, mindlessly gripping his broad shoulders while the velvet warmth of his mouth drifted tantalisingly over hers. Her senses were spinning. Slowly, as through a distant haze, she registered that she was enjoying the embrace and murmuring her appreciation.

Humiliated and unhappy, she forced herself back into the real, harsh world he'd driven her into, reached back with her hand—and slapped his face hard, slipping from his grasp before he could respond.

'You may have some mental and emotional hold over me,' she grated angrily, 'but that doesn't give you the right to maul me around whenever the fancy strikes you! You must be almost twice my age! *If* I were interested in men at this time in my life—*if*—then it certainly wouldn't be you!'

László's eyes flickered. 'Never forget that I am rooted in deep passions,' he murmured by way of an excuse. 'A mixture of Russian and Hungarian, with fire within me. It's hard for me to resist a lovely woman when she's in my arms and begging to be kissed.'

'I wasn't! And I think you'd better start trying to resist!' she ground out furiously.

'Perhaps you should keep your distance,' he suggested laconically.

'I wish we had the English Channel between us! Just control your animal feelings for the next hour or so!'

she yelled. With cold hauteur, she stalked into the castle, László close at her heels.

'There he is!' László exclaimed with satisfaction. 'Call him!'

She had no choice. 'Oh, God!' she whispered. Then; 'István!' she carolled gaily as her brother-in-law disappeared into his study.

His head appeared around the door again. His eyebrows rose when he saw how closely entwined she was with László and she felt her stomach knot with tension. When her legs buckled, László drew her even more tightly to him and István's eyes flickered with disapproval.

I can't do this! she thought desperately as her hip shifted seductively against László's. She couldn't think straight. This was going to be worse than she thought!

Yet something within her surfaced and took over. Self-preservation perhaps, or the knowledge that she had to make a good job of this if her family were to believe her commitment. Driven partly by anger at László's outrageous invasion of her life and personal space—no, her sexual space, she thought miserably, only too aware of the sinfully sexy man by her side—she took the bull by the horns and acted her heart out for the first time ever.

'Hello! Are you going soon?' she cried as amiably as she could

'Suzanne! Are you drunk?' frowned István, ready to protect her from opportunist predators.

The iron muscles warming her thigh stiffened imperceptibly. 'No!' she said indignantly, her heavy mouth sullen.

'Get him in the study,' muttered László under his breath. A firm male hand squeezed her waist in encouragement.

She took two deep breaths and flashed a carefree smile. Bearing down on István, they forced him to step back into the room and the relief of privacy. 'I wanted a private word,' she said jerkily, hearing the door shut with a thud behind them.

'Go on,' said István quietly, his eyes warily flicking from one to the other.

The moment had come. Her voice wobbled. 'I—I've come to introduce you to my financial backer——'

István relaxed and smiled wryly. 'I thought you were going to say something else,' he grinned, holding out his hand to László. 'Congratulations,' he said, while Suzanne stared at him in horror. 'You've acquired a cracker of a business deal.'

László folded his arms, his eyes like slits. 'I know,' he said softly. 'Perhaps you should tell him who I am.' She flung him a startled look of sheer panic and he shook his head at her. 'The name everyone knows me by?' he suggested, a wicked glint making his eyes shine as if he had a fever.

Suzanne let out a small moan. 'This... this is...' István's curious gaze swivelled to her. 'László,' she husked.

'Lázár,' murmured László.

Her brother-in-law went white and retracted his hand as if it had been seared by a flame-thrower. Misery engulfed her. He didn't know what a terrible decision she'd had to make. He had no idea that she was betraying him because it was her best option. He'd just think she was a materialistic bitch, selfish, with no sense of family pride! Everyone would hate her! Her hands clenched. László was pitching her against her family. How dare he divide her from them! How dare he!

'You're not to know, Sue, but this man's not welcome in my house,' growled István. 'He and I are old adversaries——'

'I do know,' she broke in curtly. 'But your affairs aren't anything to do with me.' She quailed at what she was saying. He'd think she was shallow, uncaring. Her hatred for László intensified as István's jaw dropped in amazement. 'Our business arrangement is quite settled,' she said shakily and strengthened her voice. 'He's going to finance me and introduce me to the contacts I need. I'm sure you'll put aside your differences and welcome him, for my sake.'

'Like hell I will!'

'Like hell you will,' murmured László, his voice husky and tinged with amusement.

Suzanne shot him a carefully restrained glance. Beneath his dark-fringed lashes, the sinner's eyes glittered in elation. Her hand fidgeted on her thigh, itching to hit him again and to wipe the superior, smug smile off his face. Then the fear came. He could have set this up. He'd promised that there was more to come... He might be fooling her, intending to reveal his identity before them all! Her eyes searched his frantically, noted the lifted eyebrow, the mocking smile...

CHAPTER FIVE

SUZANNE'S lips trembled. They felt as if they were coated in ashes. 'You...won't——' she croaked.

László gave a shrug. 'Depends,' he drawled. 'It's entirely up to you.'

Suzanne began to panic again, silently praying that she could pull this off. If not, he could hurt them all with one, simple sentence. And would; the cruelty of that mouth had never been more apparent than now.

'István,' she husked, her eyes huge with dismay. 'Don't make waves, for my sake!' she begged plaintively.

'Do you know what this man's done?' asked her brother-in-law. 'Quite apart from putting every obstacle in my way during those years I spent working night and day with my bare hands renovating the castle, he's a crook—corrupt, devious, and not to be trusted. You bastard!' he flung at László, and her heart somersaulted with terror. They were going to fight.

In a flash she had flung herself at István, looking up at him with pleading eyes. 'Don't do this to me!' she cried piteously. 'I—I need the money——'

'I can lend you money!' raged István. 'Dammit, Sue! We've got to talk. Alone.'

'I'll wait outside, shall I?' László said softly, and she could hear the steel blades that the silken tones sheathed.

He had the confidence of a man who held the winning cards, the nerve of a gambler, and he was enjoying this moment, relishing it to the full and her mind was murderous.

Her eyes slanted up to László's. 'Well, I——'

He patted her on the head like a dog he was fond of. 'Be a good girl and talk to your brother-in-law. He can't do anything now we've made our pact, but I expect he wants to make sure you don't get the bad end of any deals we make,' he said indulgently. And smiled at her as if she were a simpering bimbo of his.

She gave him an old-fashioned look that told him not to patronise her again and clenched her fists meaningfully. He looked down at them and chuckled. Chuckled! Inside, she came to a slow boil. She'd flatten him when they were alone!

'I'm not wet behind the ears,' she told him curtly. 'I've studied business. I read the financial sections of the quality papers and the business sections. I know exactly how much profit I need to make, what my margins should be and what my market is. If you imagine I'm going to be someone you can milk dry then you're mistaken.'

He laughed, a genuinely delighted laugh that changed his face in an instant. She felt the muscles and tendons of her pelvis contract, her body firing with hungry flames. He'd be quite irresistible, she thought hazily, if he weren't so *evil*.

'That's pretty convincing,' he said. 'But please, humour your protector. Let him lecture you.'

His challenging eyes met István's and Suzanne shivered at the pagan clash of wills. Both men were dark and intense, both passionately devoted to their beliefs. One was amused and mocking, the other hostile. But both had the same blood flowing in their veins, and the knowledge of that haunted her. Erect and haughty, they had the pride of all those with Hungarian blood—but László was concealing aces under the table and could produce them and win the game at any moment.

She felt faint with the tension chasing through her entire body and without László's soothing hand stroking her back, she would have been on her knees.

'I wouldn't dream of lecturing my sister-in-law,' answered István coldly. 'But I intend to advise her and give her some valuable information.'

'You're wasting your time,' drawled László. 'She's made her mind up.'

István's mouth thinned. 'She'll change it when she's heard what I've got to say. Who invited you here?' he asked coldly.

'I didn't need an invitation,' grated László.

Sensing he was becoming dangerously angry, Suzanne did the only thing she could think of. She turned into his body slightly and placed the flat of her hand on his chest. Smiling into his eyes, she reached up on tiptoe and kissed his angry mouth.

Her head swam. His lips had softened immediately, his gentle fingers cupping the delicate bones of her face. Wonderful. Only the tense situation drew her away, István's gasp ringing harshly in her ears.

'He—he didn't need one,' she confirmed breathily. 'He's my...' She tried to simper and hoped it looked realistic. 'My *special* guest.'

'My God! We have to talk, Sue,' muttered István through his teeth. '*You*, Lázár, will do us the courtesy of waiting outside while we do so. Sue?'

She flinched at the barked command. 'Yes,' she mumbled.

Her brother-in-law stretched out his hand to her then his eyes narrowed. 'You've torn your dress!' he said harshly, his accusing eyes going immediately to the motionless László.

'She slipped,' he explained smoothly without even a pause. 'On the grass.' He gave a mocking half-smile that infuriated her with its sensual suggestion. 'That's how we...' He hesitated and if she hadn't known him as well as she did, she would have said he'd mimicked her fluttering simper with a more masculine equivalent. 'How we got together. Isn't that right, sweetie?' he asked fondly, smiling into her eyes.

She faltered, and decided miserably that she might as well use that shudder of loathing and turn it into a feminine tremble. 'We talked for ages,' she said unsteadily.

'Among other things,' murmured László.

Blushing, she cursed him because he knew she dared not deny what he was implying. And burned with mor-

tification when László chuckled warmly and sauntered
out. The man was insensitive, she thought angrily! Thick-
skinned, inflexible and a butter-tongued liar! And she'd
make sure he regretted the way he'd handled this!

When the study door had been slammed behind her,
she attacked first. 'Before you say anything,' she said,
her pale face the colour of chalk, 'I know that László
is a rival and that you are at daggers drawn. It doesn't
make any difference to me and neither should it. He's
offered me a chance to build my business. I've assessed
it, and it's the kind of offer I can't refuse. I know you
disapprove of him——'

'That's putting it mildly,' growled István. 'He's——'

'Please, let me finish,' she interrupted. 'I have a right
to make my own business decisions——'

'Not with a cheat and a liar!' declared István passionately. 'And as far as his familiarity to you is concerned,
whatever liberties he's taken, don't let him take any
more——'

'István!' she gasped. 'How can you think——?'

'It's plain on your face!' he growled. 'I'm trying to
protect you, Sue! I care for you! Your sisters and John
would never forgive me if you came to grief in that bastard's hands!'

'I have no intention of coming to grief!' she shot, desperate to be saved from the ghastly situation. But how
could she? Inwardly she groaned and steeled herself
against his displeasure. They mustn't know she was being
forced into this course of action. 'I'm fed up with being
the baby of the family. My life is my business! Who I
kiss, who I flirt with and who I do business with is
nothing to do with anyone else! I want to do something
on my own,' she cried obstinately. 'I won't let you stop
me. I'm determined to go ahead.' She flushed scarlet at
his sharp inhalation, hating herself for upsetting him on
this day of all days. 'Your experience with László,
whatever that might be,' she went on doggedly, 'isn't
going to stop me. Sheer common sense tells me I'd be
a fool to snap my fingers at this opportunity. So don't
waste your time talking to me. I think you should leave

me to make my own decisions and stop interfering!' she finished heatedly.

'OK. You're smart where business is concerned. But you're inexperienced with men. He's——'

'Don't patronise me!' she yelled. 'I can see he's a womaniser. OK, he kisses up a storm.' She cringed at the rage in István's dark eyes and only hysterical desperation forced her on. 'I'm well aware that's because he's probably made love to more women than he can remember! And why shouldn't I enjoy his kisses? There's no law against that. I'm not going to do anything *stupid*! I have my principles. I will deal with him on a business basis and have a little fun, but I won't compromise my morals,' she said mutinously, willing her legs to stop shaking.

'You can't protect yourself against a man as wily and as determined as László,' growled István.

'Thanks for the vote of confidence,' she said sharply. She stalked to the door, hoping she looked convincingly annoyed with his interference. She had to act tough, to be defiant. Rude, if necessary. 'Let me make my own mistakes if necessary,' she muttered, with a defiant toss of her head.

'A mistake with this guy would last you a lifetime.'

Her stomach churned at the tone of tender concern and disappointment. Her suspicions about László had been confirmed. He was to be avoided at all costs. Somehow she must get out of his clutches. But not now, not yet, however much she wanted to.

'You've said your piece. Thank you for caring. Now you have a bride waiting for you,' she reminded him, her voice beginning to break up. 'Forget your worries about me. Consider your own lives and don't let this blight your pleasure in any way.' Her eyes pleaded with him. '*Please*!' she cried in heartfelt anguish.

He began to talk quietly to her, listing all the things László had done to cause him trouble, and her heart ached that István had put up with so much. 'I won't listen!' she said huskily, clapping her hands over her ears. Like the countess, she'd made a choice for the good of all—and there was no going back. 'You're upsetting me!' she cried, her eyes bright with the unshed tears. 'Don't you want me to make it on my own? You have no *right*!' she wailed.

'That man has some crazy power complex,' István muttered. 'He's been trying to ruin my life ever since I returned to Hungary after discovering my inheritance. He could be getting at me through you——'

László had reason to hate and hurt them all, she thought raggedly. And probably would, unless she could control him in some way. A tear escaped at last and trickled down her cheek. István gave a concerned cry and moved forward but she cringed against the door.

'Leave me alone!' she sobbed. 'Do you want everyone to hear me crying and come in here and see that there's a rift between us? Do you want Tanya to be upset on her wedding-day? All he wants is to make a profit out of me. I beg you, let me do this. It's my life. I'm over twenty-one!'

István slammed his hand on the desk as if intending to fight her every inch of the way. 'You mustn't sign anything without our lawyers checking first for loopholes. God, Sue,' he groaned. 'Why are you so stubborn?'

'My dream colours my life,' she whispered. Gathering her remaining strength, she forced a quaveringly bright smile. 'I can keep a clear head,' she assured him, pushing aside the memory of her temporary insanity when László had kissed her. 'I can't come to that much harm, can I?'

Again he argued, a cruelly gentle, loving argument, that hurt her more than any outright battle. But she held firm, knowing that time was on her side. He would have to leave for his honeymoon very soon.

And when she was almost at the end of her tether, he capitulated at last, giving her one final, stiffly worded warning to take care, reminding her that he was on the end of a phone any time she wanted help—any time at all, day or night.

To her unutterable relief, the first part was over. She hoped it would prove to be the worst she had to endure but didn't feel inclined to put bets on it. She went weak at the knees thinking of spending the next few weeks in László's unnerving company.

When she entered the hall she noticed that the main door was open and the family were saying their goodbyes. László was a half-seen shadow on the edge of darkness. As she came closer, trying to remain concealed so that she could watch him unobserved, she could see the stillness that he wore like a cloak. She saw also the shrewd, constant flickering of his perceptive eyes as he noted every gesture, every word and slight body movement that might give him clues to the feelings of his... She gulped. His relatives.

He'd see affection and love between them all, she thought. Then wondered if that would anger him more because he should be part of this family group and yet had been excluded by a cruel fate.

Her hand went to her throat. He was watching the countess, every tiny move she made, every graceful gesture of her aristocratic body. It was obvious from the way he blindly gripped the rough stem of the potted palm that, whatever he'd pretended, seeing his mother—and remaining a stranger to her—was racking him with a heart-wrenching pain.

The dark face was raw with anguish that seemed to punch her in the stomach with a breath-destroying force. Feeling wretched, she peered more keenly into the murky shadows and saw the sensual, kissable mouth had thinned to a whitened slash from the rigid control he must be exerting on himself. His eyes looked bleak, the mocking and amused light that had glowed there earlier now totally extinguished.

And the vigour that had energised him and brought her to life had totally gone and she had a glimpse of his emptiness, the sorrow that lay inside him and had grown and swollen with the years in a cancerous core. He'd suffered, there was no doubt of that. But he wanted the people she loved to suffer too, to become infected with his disease, to live with bitterness and disharmony like him.

An eye for an eye, a tooth for a tooth, she thought, appalled.

Yet . . . although she didn't wish him well, nevertheless it touched her heart to know that he did feel despair because his mother had rejected him. It was a terrible situation. Sadly Suzanne imagined the countess's distress on learning that she was carrying Nikolai's child; her instinctive distaste at the thought of anyone with Russian blood inheriting her home, and her terrible state of mind when László was born and she found she couldn't, wouldn't love him.

An image came strongly to her of the baby László screaming for attention and no one daring to pick him up because they'd risk the wrath of the distraught countess. She tried to think what it must be like to live for years with a man you hated and knew she could never have done that—the sacrifice would have been too great, even for a thousand-year-old dynasty.

But she couldn't bear the thought of the child crying, either, not even for a day. László had been fed stories of hatred, too, she mused. He and his father had been hurt so deeply that László had felt compelled to take some kind of revenge, if only for his father's sake.

And she'd been dragged into the middle of a maelstrom.

Seeing László's silent, secret grief made a difference to her feelings for him. It wasn't his fault that he was the heir—or that his father had been reviled by the countess. How awful that must feel, to know you were an unwanted child! The thought tore her in two and she gave an involuntary sigh at the tragedy of it all.

His tragic expression immediately went blank. His sharp eyes flicked over to her immediately. With typical pinpoint accuracy, he sought her out from the huge display of flowers that almost concealed her and beckoned with his expressive hand.

'Tomorrow, it begins,' he said in an undertone, when she reluctantly came over to him. 'Ten o'clock. I'll pick you up and we'll spend the day together.'

Her heart thudded wildly. He was projecting every ounce of his sexuality again and a *frisson* of awareness had rendered her body despairingly receptive. Her hesitation made him raise an eyebrow and glance meaningfully at the happy family group.

'All right,' she whispered hoarsely.

'I look forward to it,' he husked. The dark lashes fluttered. His lips moved gently against hers, all too briefly.

Her eyes wouldn't open. He'd drugged her. There was no resistance in her body, only a longing to be gathered in his arms. A small pulse beat at her throat and was driven crazy by his gentle kiss, then she felt the erotic tug of his teeth on her pouting lower lip and, after that, a terrible void.

He'd gone. Her hands clasped the trunk of the palm as though it might save her from falling. In the background, she heard the familiar slam of the study door and jerked into life. István emerged and headed, grim-faced, for Vigadó. She groaned. They mustn't discuss her!

Feeling a lying fraud, she ran to István and hugged him before he was halfway across the hall. 'I'm so happy!' she cried fervently. And strangely, she was, wanting to sing and dance, a wonderful warm feeling seeping through her entire body. László, she thought muzzily. It was all in his kisses, his caress.

'You don't know what this means to me,' she said, her voice shaking with emotion. 'I've worked for this moment all my life. Don't tell anyone else, I beg you! The recriminations will delay your departure. Promise? For Tanya's sake? We both love her too much... Oh, please, please, promise!'

'Damn you! Take care,' husked István, moved by her plea. 'Trust nothing he says, nothing he does. Here's my number at the hotel. I'll fly back at a moment's notice if you need me. Tanya will understand. For God's sake!'

he urged, 'reconsider, don't let your ambition blind you to this man's ruthless and underhand character!'

'Go on!' she said shakily. 'I'll protect myself. I swear I won't let him hurt you by compromising me.'

He smiled gently and kissed her brow. Feeling like howling, she flung her arms around Tanya, Lisa and John. 'Goodbye! Goodbye!' she cried. 'Have lovely, lovely honeymoons!'

And her pleading, liquid green eyes begged István not to say anything, or cause Tanya any misgivings. When the tail-lights had vanished down the brazier-lined driveway, she glanced over to the shadows but saw only darkness. And wearily said goodnight to the others and went slowly up to bed.

Exhaustion didn't help her to sleep. All night the seductive, smouldering eyes haunted her thoughts. The reason for that was incomprehensible. Perhaps it was the menace they'd projected, the sense of danger.

Admittedly he was better-looking than any other man she'd known. He was mature too, with none of the irritatingly gauche approaches she'd endured from would-be boyfriends before. Also, she reasoned gloomily, he'd probably spent a lifetime enchanting women and driving them mad.

Suzanne rolled over and plumped up the broderie anglaise pillow then threw off the thin sheet that covered her naked body. The cool air took some of the heat from her skin but she still felt more sensual, more womanly than in the whole of her life.

The worst thing, she thought morosely, trying to stifle the sinful craving for László's intoxicating kisses, was that he knew what he was doing to her. She extended her body like a cat and her traitorous mind instantly placed László there beside her, his hands shaping her curves as she stretched on the inviting bed.

Shame made her hastily whip the sheet up to cover herself again and she mortified her flesh by curling up, tensing every muscle and thinking of intricate patterns, machine oil, wads of money and, filled with desperation that László still occupied her thoughts, she visualised him at home in check carpet slippers, a grey cardy and corduroy trousers.

It helped. For a start, it brought a smile to her face. The man was mortal! she grinned ruefully. And vowed to bring that image up every time she was in trouble.

'Stunning.'

Her stomach did its familiar victory roll but she held her gaze steady. 'Isn't it!' she said with satisfaction, patting her glossy Mexican-style bun. Despite her languid gesture, she was secretly devouring the sharp lines of his beautifully tailored navy suit in a summerweight linen. He looked absolutely devastating.

'Shall we go?' he murmured.

Her eyes flicked to the black convertible and back. 'Where?' And gritted her teeth because her nerves were all over the place at the thought of spending time close to him.

The teasing eyes simmered lazily. 'First to discuss plans and strategies, then to textile co-operatives,' he drawled, opening the passenger door for her.

'What fun!' she declared. But her hand shook in his when he handed her in and she felt appalled that he should affect her so easily. Carpet slippers, she said to herself. And smiled secretly.

László slid his lithe body into the driver's seat and turned his body to face her, one arm resting along the back of his seat. Without hurrying, he examined her from head to toe, totally unaware of her silent chant about slippers and woolly cardis.

'I can put the top up if you like. I wouldn't like your lovely hair to be spoiled,' he suggested, caressing her with his eyes.

'No, please don't,' she said quickly. 'I love the wind on my face and my hair can be easily tamed.' Seeing the quiver of his lips, she added, 'unlike me.'

'Or me,' he told her. 'That makes our relationship more exciting, doesn't it?'

'All we have in common,' she answered coldly, 'is an interest in making a profit.'

'A little more than that, I think. We've chosen the same shade of navy for our suits,' he remarked idly. That fact hadn't escaped her. Or the white shirts. The sharp contrast of his tanned throat and snowy collar made him look impeccably groomed and even more striking than she recalled. 'You look very efficient,' he continued.

'I am.'

'Beautifully turned out, cool, enough make-up to suggest you've bothered, not too much to detract from your wish to appear businesslike. Sufficient height to your heels to add some command, not too much that you lose the practicality of comfort for the long day ahead.'

'What long day?' she asked warily, a little astonished that he'd listed all the points that had gone through her own mind when she was deciding on her outfit. They thought alike, knew the importance of detail in personal presentation. How odd.

'We have a lot to talk about and the co-operatives are rather spread about,' he replied with a faintly worrying smoothness.

'I have to be back here for dinner,' she said sharply.

László inclined his head. 'As you wish.' He started the car and they drove through the gates and into the village.

Suzanne had wondered if he would look up at the castle windows for a glimpse of his mother, but perhaps he'd done that while he was waiting. It was so tragic that they'd never know one another and come to terms with what had happened. If they could only meet, maybe the bitterness would go. Perhaps she could get them together so they could get to know one another slowly, she thought. They'd like each other and begin to trust one another and... A lump came into her throat, the sympathy she felt quite impossible to keep down.

'You must have felt odd last night,' she said soberly, 'going home after being here.'

'I didn't go home.'

He'd slipped on a pair of sunglasses and she couldn't see behind the black mirrors that reflected her distorted, pale face. But in his tone she'd heard a slight wavering huskiness and she felt sad that life was never simple and straightforward. Then she realised a flaw in his statement.

'You changed your suit,' she said tartly. 'Did you find it on a convenient bush?'

'My hotel.'

'Oh!' She subsided, chastened by his curtness, and stared at the colourful village houses. Wrought-iron railings, painted in blues and greens, protected small, luxuriant flower gardens from the herds of cattle which were driven through daily. In the summer heat, women were busy watering the gardens while their children played underfoot.

She checked László's expression. He too was eyeing the family life; the man, hand in hand with his little daughter, the children skipping by the church, the laughing woman who swept her son into her arms and whirled the squealing child around in the air. All this must hurt, she mused. These were *his* villagers.

'Is your home a long way away, then?' she asked gently.

László gave an expressive shrug. 'My home is wherever I lay my head. I virtually live out of a suitcase. No ties, no responsibilities. Manhattan, Knightsbridge, Hong Kong, Milan, Budapest.'

Her eyes dropped to the strong hand, deftly changing gear. He wore an expensive gold ring on the third finger of his left hand which she hadn't noticed before and his cufflinks were sapphire studs. The watch, however, was cheap and workmanlike. Forgetting why she'd begun to assess his worth, she digested the fact that he'd not worn the ring the previous night. He must be married or divorced. No—not divorced; he'd have dumped the ring without a qualm if so. A wife! She tried to imagine what the woman was like. Perfect. Glamorous and sophisticated. No wonder István had been alarmed at László's behaviour—and hers—last night!

'You puzzle me,' she said slowly. She hesitated, something stopping her from asking about his wife and the possible existence of a family. He'd think she was fishing. 'If you're so rich,' she substituted, 'why don't you have a grand home to put all your possessions in?'

He laughed as if the idea were ridiculous and increased speed so that the wind whipped his hair and lent a carefree manner to his appearance. 'I have no possessions,' he said surprisingly. 'And I don't want a grand home—or anything else that would clip my wings.' He glanced at her, savouring the lines of her body with a dizzyingly heady appreciation. 'The moment you possess something,' he said softly, 'you are vulnerable. And I have learnt the danger of that condition.'

'Is that why you don't want Kastély Huszár?' she asked shrewdly, hoping to force him to show his hand.

'A contributing factor,' he drawled.

'Explain,' she demanded abruptly. 'Tell me why you don't want a title and estates. It's a little difficult to believe, to be honest.'

'Have you any idea what it means to own a large house, vast estates and to be responsible for a whole raft of villagers?' he asked incredulously. 'Think of it. The long-term responsibility is a burden. As the count, I'd have to be concerned with the minutiae of everyone's life. It would be a weight around my neck and I'd have no time to travel or enjoy the fast cut and thrust of making deals around the world and beating my competitors at their own game. I'm a restless man. I don't like getting bogged down. I take my pleasures on the hoof.'

'The wild ponies,' she said to herself softly.

But he'd heard. 'I think you'll find I'm classified as a stallion.'

Suzanne coloured scarlet. 'You might become reconciled with your mother,' she suggested quietly, remembering his longing the night before. 'Wouldn't you like that?'

'The cost would be too great,' he muttered grimly. 'Even if I did want that. Why did you bring the matter up?' he asked, frowning. 'Surely you have a vested interest in keeping me away from the countess?'

'Yes, but I have to know for certain that you really would prefer to keep your identity secret,' she replied soberly. 'I've thought about my situation carefully. It would be unwise of me to tie myself up legally with you, only to discover that your real intention was to take over the castle come what may.'

'I told you. I don't want it. I'm rich enough to have all the money I want, to buy a far larger estate than that of the Huszárs——' he began, his pride obviously dented.

'But that's not the point,' she insisted. However risky it might be, she had to push him to the limit. She must know how set he was on keeping his side of the bargain. 'There's a dynasty involved that goes back a long, long way and you're part of that bloodline. Don't you feel anything for it?'

'No.'

'You're lying!' she accused, seeing how tightly he was clenching the wheel. And they were travelling far too fast for the narrowness of the road.

His mouth twisted. 'A man has to protect his emotions,' he muttered.

'Why?'

'Blunt as ever!' he said with a small laugh. His foot eased up on the accelerator and she breathed a sigh of relief. 'Giving way to emotions means committing yourself. I prefer to run free. I've been content up to now with the knowledge that the woman who cheated on her part of the bargain with my father has been desperately unhappy. She took a lover but she had little joy of him. She sacrificed herself to earth and stone and mortar—and paid the price: a lifetime without love—apart from a brief tumble in the hay.'

Suzanne bristled. 'She's a deeply loving woman,' she began passionately.

'Now she might be—because she's realised at last that property is no substitute for people,' he said harshly. 'It's a little late for me, her son, though, isn't it? She took a long time to learn that possessions are ephemeral. You can lose them by force of circumstance. Only strong,

loving relationships carry you through times of hardship
and help you to survive them.'

'If you know that, then you must have had a good
childhood,' she ventured, fervently agreeing with him.
He could love. She felt glad. And a glimmer of hope
came into her mind. Anyone who had the capacity to
love could show compassion, given time.

'I was loved,' he said fondly.

'But it wasn't enough, was it?' she said huskily. 'You
wanted the love of your mother as well.'

The softened mouth thinned. 'Is that what you think?
You want to know the truth? When I began to make
enquiries about the Huszár fortunes and I heard that she
had nothing but a ramshackle cottage and the rags she
stood up in, I was glad. I went out and celebrated.' He
gave a cruel and ironic laugh. 'Despite her noble sacrifice, despite selling her soul to the man she'd called
the devil incarnate, the castle had fallen into decay and
the land was run down and worthless. I can assure you,'
he said harshly, 'that gave me an immense satisfaction.'

'But the situation changed when István returned,' she
said quietly. 'He began to renovate the castle and give
it life again.' Remembering what she'd been told, she
decided to test his honesty. 'That must have annoyed
you. What did you do then?'

'I made life as difficult as I could for him,' he said
calmly. 'I did my best to make sure that deliveries were
never made, stone-masons and craftsmen were diverted
by the simple means of offering better paid work elsewhere, government officials were persuaded to refuse
permissions. And I made sure that István knew who was
behind all his problems.'

Suzanne felt her spine chill. 'That was unnecessarily
vindictive,' she said coldly.

He gave a careless shrug of his tailored shoulders.
'What was I to do? Allow them a fairy-tale ending?' he
said sardonically. 'I know myself well enough to realise
that I needed to feel I was avenging my father somehow,
or my anger would have festered until it couldn't be contained any longer—and I'd be storming up the drive with

writs in my hand and proofs of my inheritance. I prefer the slow burn,' he said in a sexy drawl. 'Prolonged torture, the infliction of a thousand wounds.'

She shifted uncomfortably in the contoured leather seat. That could still happen, with the next stage of his revenge to come. The knowledge hung over her like the sword of Damocles, ready to fall and split her in two. She must play a dangerous game of placating László and yet not letting him walk all over her. Deliberately she steadied her breathing and made herself sound relaxed.

'However much you tried, you didn't succeeed in your vendetta against István,' she observed, proud of her brother-in-law's persistance and determination. 'He overcame all the difficulties you created and restored the estate beautifully.' But as soon as she'd said that, she felt the pain László must have experienced when he'd walked around the castle and the grounds during the wedding party and wondered again why she should care that he suffered when he cared for no one other than himself.

'He did,' agreed László, his mouth hard. 'Haven't you ever heard of the cruel trick of letting someone think they've reached calmer waters, before sinking their ship? Life won't be easy for him from now on.'

'What do you mean by that?' she demanded warily.

'Can you imagine how he feels now? His arch rival has financed his sister-in-law. And apparently captured her interest, too. He'll be worrying about that and it'll be taking some of the joy out of his honeymoon,' he drawled. 'And he knows my methods well enough to re-alise that I probably struck up a . . .' His mouth twitched in amusement. 'A relationship, on purpose, just to annoy him.'

Suzanne felt insulted. He'd kissed her because he wanted to get back at István. Not because he'd wanted to. She flushed. Of course, since he was married she didn't *want* his attentions. But it was humiliating to be used so blatantly. 'Then he'll realise you don't mean anything by it,' she said haughtily.

'Of course he will. Long ago he formed the opinion that I have a steel-clad pump instead of a heart,' he murmured. 'Every time he touches your sister, he could be thinking of you and me together. He'll be afraid that I'm intending to go as far as I can with you, just for the pleasure of revenge,' he husked. His hand ran up her leg, pushing beneath the hem of her skirt and she slapped it away angrily. 'That kind of thing can be very emasculating.' He grinned. 'I hope I didn't spoil his wedding-night,' he mused.

'Oh!' she gasped, realising the extent of the repercussions. 'Tanya might have spent the whole night in tears! You brute! I never thought...! Don't you have any human feeling?' she wailed. Her angry eyes scalded his. 'You really are a deeply unpleasant man!' she grated, wishing she could ring István and reassure him.

László's jaw tightened. 'I'm dealing with unpleasant matters,' he growled. 'Everyone defends the world they've created. I'm defending mine—and I'll defend it to the death.' Suzanne shivered at the feral mutter. 'I told you that I have a deal to make.' His mouth thinned to a grim, determined line. 'It would be to my advantage if I had something very, very special to bargain with.'

She saw his cold, contemptuous eyes on her and interpreted their calculated assessment. 'Me,' she breathed. 'You mean to use me as a bargaining tool in—in some other way than you said! What are you going to do? Where are we going? Stop the car! I want to get out!' she cried hysterically. '*Stop it, I say!*'

CHAPTER SIX

THE car swerved and Suzanne screamed as he grimly brought it under control. 'Don't be a fool,' he said irritably. 'Stop trying to kill us. We have work to do.'

He patted her knee. She shifted her leg to one side and he pulled it back, sliding his hand over the silky stocking till she felt the rhythm deep inside her. 'I want a cast-iron guarantee from you,' she muttered grimly, gritting her teeth against the pleasure of his touch.

'We've agreed on the basis of our relationship,' he said lazily, his eyes flicking to the driving mirror.

'I know,' she said shakily. 'You play fair with me and I'll play fair with you.'

'Oh, dear,' he drawled. 'I wasn't planning on anything so delightfully old-fashioned.'

She opened her mouth indignantly and then realised he was slowing the car and drawing in to a lay-by. 'What are you doing now?' she demanded suspiciously when he turned off the engine.

'I need a coffee,' he said with an innocent look, and pointed to the Büfé, one of the little kiosks serving snacks that were positioned at regular intervals along Hungarian roads. 'And besides,' he added, leaning over confidentially, 'we're being followed.'

'What——?'

'Don't turn around!' he warned, as her head jerked in shocked surprise. His fingers caught her jaw. 'In case you're wondering, I'm doing this to allay their suspicions,' he said, kissing her warmly. His amused eyes searched hers. 'And because it's a wonderful way to spend a summer morning,' he added insolently, his mouth descending again.

She struggled to hate it. But the more he kissed her, the more she enjoyed it. There was a satin feel to his

91

mouth, a firmness, that gave her a deep, abiding pleasure which flowed into her very bones and made her feel good. Gradually, to her horror, she began to sink beneath his onslaught, her resistance becoming feeble and half-hearted.

'Suzanne,' he sighed into her mouth.

'Don't——' She wriggled ineffectually and moaned in helpless dismay, trapped by his weight. He had eased a hand beneath her jacket and was already sliding it to cup her breast, exploring its fullness, teasing the firm centre to even greater tension than before.

'Suzanne,' he muttered harshly again.

The longing in his voice sent shudders through her body. Deep and slow, his mouth moved over hers, arousing them both. Fighting him all the way, she was acutely aware of the erratic thud of his heart beneath her protesting palm, the sound of his rapid, shallow breathing. And his fingers worked an unwelcome magic on her lifting breast, inflaming her passions till she threw her head back in despair and thus suffered the sensual stroking of his tongue along her vulnerable throat. It made her feel...voluptuous. Sensual. Desirable.

For a moment she could do nothing, only savour the sensations. His velvet-smooth cheek sliding over hers. The silk of his beautiful hair and the warm scalp beneath her fingertips. The long, black fringe of lashes concealing the glittering eyes...only now they were smouldering with desire. And the muted growl in his throat as he repeatedly kissed her was driving her insane.

He began to draw away. For one awful moment, her fingers tightened on his neck—how, she wondered briefly, had they got there?—and then common sense reasserted itself in her crazy head and she pulled back, her eyes huge, with dark, forest green lights glowing in the molten brown.

'László!' she breathed huskily. 'How dare——?'

'I think that was long enough to be convincing,' he drawled. 'You struggled surprisingly well. Nicely done. Now slap my face.'

'What?' she mumbled, her head still treacherously somewhere on Cloud Nine.

His mouth found hers again, hard and ruthless, but this time he whispered against her open lips, the gentle heat of each word filling her mouth with sensation, 'István and Vigadó will send out the troops if they think I've succeeded in seducing you.' His tongue tasted the softness of her inner lip. 'We don't want their interference. I know your seduction is becoming something of a pleasant reality, but——'

Wrenching herself free, she did just what he'd asked. Her hand connected violently with his face and she felt a deep satisfaction in the hard stinging sensation that remained on her palm. The slap relieved some of her fierce feelings, too. 'You—you——!' she spluttered.

'Sorry! Sorry!' he fended, holding up his hands. 'Forgive me, I went too far!' He lowered his voice. 'Well done. I had to provoke you, Suzanne. That had the desired effect, I think!'

'Are you playing to the gallery or apologising?' she bit.

'Both?' he suggested, vastly amused. 'Apply a little of your famous logic to the situation, Suzanne. If you want Big-Brother-in-law checking your every movement, then let them know you've succumbed to me. If not— and I take it you don't want his interference any more than I do—you must prove you can handle me on your own. I'm honour bound by my reputation as a first-class lecher to make a play for you. It would be surprising if I didn't. Therefore I must be seen to kiss you and you must be seen to slap me down.'

She wondered if that was really what he'd been doing. 'I don't believe anyone's following us!' she muttered.

He angled he driving mirror towards her. 'Pretend to be checking your make-up and take a look at the car that's just drawn up,' he said calmly.

Suzanne angrily pushed her shirt into her waistband, did up the jacket buttons that he'd undone with the skill of the pickpocket Fagin, and scowled at her startled-rabbit reflection. Apart from looking as though she'd

been thoroughly dazzled, she seemed to have about
fourteen thumbs on the ends of her hands. He was far
too calm! Her hand paused in the fumbling action of
tucking back a strand of hair behind her ears.

'The Mercedes——!' she began in surprise, recognising the car immediately.

'I know. It's István's,' he said laconically.

So he *had* been fondling her for a reason. Calculating
beast! 'How did *you* know it's his?' she muttered.

'I made sure I checked over the contents of his garages
when I first arrived. Precautions,' he said mockingly,
when her disbelieving eyes queried this. 'I think of
everything. I always believe that if you do the
groundwork and set the foundations then you can build
what you like, as high as you like. Foresight. That's what
makes me better than any man at what I do.'

'Modest, too,' she scathed.

'I put twenty per cent more effort into my life than
most people and get results. I don't believe in wasting
time denying the truth,' he said with a shrug.

'Yes, you do! You pretend that you're not hurt by
your mother's rejection,' she countered icily, re-applying
her lipstick.

'Touché.' Wincing, László pushed a tidying hand
through his tousled hair, his eyes briefly clouded. She
felt ashamed. It had been a cheap barb and it had
wounded him more than she'd imagined. But he recovered quickly. 'Nice kissing you, Suzanne. Must do it
again.'

'You will not!' she said vehemently.

He smiled the 'wait and see' kind of smile. She retaliated with a 'don't hold your breath' one that made
his sardonic features break into a slow grin.

'Shall we have a coffee and give our two "tails" the
run-around?' he suggested wickedly.

She watched him come around to her side of the car
and open the door. A little unsteadily she stood up and
was immediately clasped beneath the elbow, making her
furious that he'd correctly gauged the fact that she felt
wobbly from his kisses.

'Why are they following us and why don't we invite them to travel in our car and save petrol?' she suggested rebelliously.

László raised an arching eyebrow. 'Why? If you think István would ever have washed his hands of you and allowed you to wander around Hungary with a rake like me, then you must be barking mad!'

She stiffened and shot him a crushing glance. 'I'm not amused,' she snapped. 'If you're saying he never intended to trust me to strike out alone, then I'm very angry with him. I don't like his bossy protection. Touch me again and I'll——'

'Enjoy it even more?' he suggested insultingly.

Waves of shame flooded through her. The truth was painful to accept. 'I'll find a way to make you regret it,' she finished furiously.

'Have a sandwich,' he said consolingly.

'Do they slice and crush male egos here?' she asked sourly.

Laughing, he shook his head. 'You're quite wonderful,' he murmured. 'I am enjoying this. And so, I'm delighted to say, are you.'

She paused. Honest to a fault, she had to admit that she loved to be touched by him, to be kissed. She enjoyed being with him when she forgot the fact that he was blackmailing her. Even that she could understand. He'd been deprived of his birthright. She only wished that she could find a solution to the dilemma which would satisfy all parties. Until then, she must stay afloat and not let him sink her. Her troubled eyes lifted to his and found his solemn gaze fixed intently on her.

'I'm enjoying the thought that one day I'm going to show everyone, including you, that I can stand on my own feet——' she began.

'Not after I've kissed you, you can't,' he murmured.

Suzanne forced herself to smile. It would need a considerable amount of devious behaviour to get the better of László Huszár. 'Perhaps I'm deliberately flattering you,' she said in a low, conspiratorial undertone. And flashed him a direct, challenging glance. He'd narrowed his eyes as if he wasn't sure of her any more and she felt herself swell with triumph. 'Take care, László,' she said casually. 'I may be playing your game and assuming a weakness I don't possess. The stakes are high enough, after all. It would give me a great deal of satisfaction to see you brought to heel.'

'It would give me a fair amount to watch you try!' A feral glitter in the darkness of his gaze put her on her guard. 'But you don't have my killer instinct,' he said softly. 'You are soft, tender, sweetened by family love——'

'My family have the reputation of identifying their goals and heading in the right direction come what may,' she replied coldly. 'And if you step in my path, I will walk right over you. Don't ever forget that. I want my business. You can help me get it. For the time being, I'll go along with you. But push me too hard in *your* direction and I'll cut loose and make it on my own. Is that clear?'

'Your brother-in-law's henchmen are coming over,' he warned. 'We must make sure we allay their fears or he'll come rushing back from his honeymoon to defend your honour and your business judgement. Can't have him ruining Tanya's holiday, can we? Or treating you like a new kid sister whose ears need washing.'

Suzanne glowered at him. He knew that she'd want István to believe that she was handling the situation with aplomb. 'Coffee,' she said briskly, as though she was managing to brush off her encounter with László's mouth as something quite inconsequential. 'Two doughnuts and a sausage for me, and you're paying.'

László laughed. 'I like your nerve and abhor your diet,' he murmured drily under his breath. But he gave the order and they stood by the counter while the two men from the Mercedes lounged around and tried to look casual while listening in to their conversation. 'All right, all right,' he said, raising his voice slightly. 'I agree to your terms.' Suzanne looked at him suspiciously and saw a devil lurking in his eyes. 'I won't harass you any more,' he sighed, raising his hands in defeat. 'Your acid tongue would emasculate me for life! But...I'm taking a big risk in offering you unlimited funds. So I'm sticking out for fifty per cent of your profit in return.'

'Fifty——!' she spluttered.

'Agree!' he muttered under his breath. 'They'll all know I wouldn't settle for less. Let's just get these guys off our backs!'

'Never fifty!' she protested. 'Ten.'

László frowned. 'You want to see a new count at the castle?' he growled. Then a little louder, 'Forty per cent and that's it. I walk away.'

His cold eyes relayed to her the information that he wasn't joking. It was evidently a matter of commercial pride for him not to be undercut too much by a woman. She shrugged. What did it matter? There was no one around to hold her to her word. They were only playing a game to get rid of the men.

'Forty it is,' she said briskly, and found her hand being shaken.

'For appearance's sake,' murmured László.

But she felt some alarm and wondered if that were so and what the legal situation was in a case like this. She could claim blackmail, undue pressure. She bit her lip, worrying that she'd just verbally passed over a large portion of her profits to László.

Pretending to brush crumbs from his jacket, she murmured, 'Hold me to that bit of play-acting and I'll take you to the High Court.'

'In that case, I'd better give you directions,' he whispered back.

And to her astonishment, he went over to the two men and shook their hands.

Appalled at what she was seeing, she cringed against the snack-bar counter, the doughnut forgotten in her limp fingers. He knew them. He was talking to them like...like a friend. They were laughing. And now...

'László' she cried hoarsely, her eyes fixed in shock on the pocket tape recorder that had been produced from under one of the men's jackets.

'Forty per cent,' László called triumphantly back to her. And smiled his dazzling, sunny smile.

She froze. Only her eyes moved; watching the men slap László on the back, enjoying the joke and then stroll back to the Mercedes, ignoring her completely. He'd tricked her! she thought, her mouth dry with horror.

Suddenly she leapt into action, whirling around and flying like the wind towards the convertible. He'd left the key in the ignition. If she could get there... Oh, God! she wailed inside, hearing him pounding after her.

And she felt herself being swung around then slammed against the side of the car. Her fists came up and she beat them like hammers on his iron-hard chest but he merely laughed softly and caught her wrists, effortlessly twisting her arms behind her back.

'You evil, vicious, lying bastard!' she raged heatedly. 'They weren't István's men—they were your *friends*!'

'They work for me,' he corrected smugly. His cynical eyes glittered with relish. 'You've just learnt a very valuable business lesson,' he drawled, shifting his thighs hard against her to hold her still. 'I'm delighted to be responsible for your initiation. You were so sure of yourself,' he mocked. 'So certain that you could handle me! But you made the mistake of trusting me, of acting without thinking. Terrible, isn't it, being disillusioned? And now you're even more in my power than before.'

'No!' she moaned, aghast at her stupidity.

'Suzanne, I wheel and deal around the world. You'll meet many like me in your life. Perhaps none as ruthless,' he acknowledged, his mouth mobile with amusement at her expense. 'But it's a hard world out there and you must know that and live by hard codes before you take on responsibility for a business that employs others. Or you won't survive. You'll go under like a drowning rat.'

'But... it was István's car!' she breathed.

'Yes. However, I took the keys from the rack in the kitchens. In fact,' he said, 'I took the keys to all the vehicles—otherwise I'm certain we would have been followed and it was essential that I prevent that. I knew he'd never leave you in my clutches and I wasn't prepared to have his heavies breathing down my neck. My, oh, my, whoever he asked to follow us must be frantic,' he mused, wicked lights dancing in his daredevil eyes.

She felt the colour drain from her face. This man operated from the gutter and kept his brain in sewers. 'What you did in extracting that agreement from me won't hold up legally——' she began haughtily.

'It will. You agreed, we shook hands, it's all on tape. I would bring all my lawyers to bear on the matter if you should choose to fight,' he purred. 'At the very least, the case would show you to be a fool. Your family's fears for your business survival would be justified.'

'Ohhhh!' she growled, furious with herself. She wanted to weep with anger. 'I believed you!' she rasped, her eyes green with temper. She wrestled with him to no avail, frantically casting a panic-stricken glance at the snack bar. They were out of sight, but she could yell and bring help if necessary. Her head jerked back again. 'I won't do business with you at all!' she cried miserably. 'I'll manage alone...'

Her voice was cut off. He was stroking her face, hunger on his lips. 'I think I should remind you of one or two facts,' he murmured. 'First, I can destroy your sister's life by a word.'

'You said you wouldn't——' she gasped out.

'Don't forget that point!' he snarled, brushing her protest aside. 'Second. I have evidence of your agreement to my share in your proposed business. Since this is a fact, you might as well make me work for it and let me set up your contacts. The success of your business would be mine too, don't forget.' His eyes pinned her like a butterfly and she found it impossible to concentrate; but somewhere washed up the dreadful thought that something was badly wrong. He wouldn't help her like this without a darker motive and that made her shake uncontrollably. 'Third,' he continued in a conversational tone.

There was more? She watched wide-eyed while he licked his lips in contemplation of her moistly parted mouth. 'Third?' she croaked.

'I'm stronger than you are. I point that out because it has a direct bearing on the fact that right at this moment, I want to make love to you and we both know that I could have you any time I chose.'

Suzanne's eyes widened even more, the bones of her face standing out in strain. 'I don't have such easy morals! If you need sex, go to your wife,' she told him shakily.

'I can't. She died four years ago.'

Widowed. Her mind tried to focus on that point. It explained his rampant sexual hunger. But it had told her nothing about his feelings for his wife. There had been no emotion, no give-away tremor in his voice, not even indifference. Just a flat monotone.

'I think,' she said tightly, 'if you try to force yourself on me, I'd be able to attract the attention of the man serving in the Büfé.'

'Possibly,' he said with a wolfish grin. His hands pressed her into his body and she quivered at its firmly toned muscles, the heat centred on the hard thrust of his pelvis.

'I reject sex with you out of hand!' she seethed.

'I wouldn't take bets on that,' he mocked. 'You're in a no-win situation and the dice are loaded in my favour. When I tie up a deal, I make sure there's plenty of string. This is it—and I must confess, I'm not sure which option I want you to choose. My head says one, my body says another...'

'What...option?' she rasped.

'Pay me forty per cent of your profits, or surrender your lips, your beautiful body, your whole self to me, willingly and without complaint.'

The wind rustled in the tall poplars that lined the road and rippled through the field of sunflowers behind her. She felt weak with the utter ruthlessness of the offer. 'My body's not for bargaining with like some medieval form of barter!' she husked.

'OK. I'll accept the percentage instead.' He must have seen the haunted look on her face and the glimmer of frustrated tears in her eyes because his tone softened a little. 'Don't take it too hard,' he murmured. 'No one's ever got the better of me yet. You'd be quite remarkable if you'd managed to do so.'

She lowered her eyes. Forty per cent! Idiot, idiot, idiot! Her mouth became grim. OK, she was beaten—for now. But, she vowed, she'd find a way, somehow, some time, to pay him back for the grief he was giving her right now when she so badly needed to feel confident and in control!

'You're too clever for me,' she muttered, sounding suitably subdued. What a fool she'd been! She *would* get the better of him, and claw back her pride! 'I accept your diagnosis. I'm too trusting.' She bit back her fury and tried to look defeated. It wasn't too hard. She felt a total failure. But he'd succeeded in making her tighten up her defences against him. 'You've accepted that this is a business relationship,' she said curtly. 'You'll have to help me if we're to be partners. I have talent, you have money. I'll stick to what I know best in future.'

Looking up from under her lashes, she caught a flash of sardonic amusement in his eyes. He felt secure in her wimpish acceptance of defeat! Her jaw clenched. Revenge would be sweet, she thought, pledging herself to victory.

The faster they drove, the more László relaxed. She could feel his body easing, the tension flowing out of him. And producing something more dangerous than his sharply tuned and devious business mind: a sensual lassitude and a smoky singing voice that reached deep into her vulnerable body.

For a while she sat taut and angry, but the wind against her face and the sensation of speed on the open road was wonderful and began to work its magic on her too.

Fields packed with maize flew by, serried rows of poplar trees whispering overhead and giving welcome shelter from the burning sun. The whitewashed long-houses and onion-topped churches gave way to more solid, Austrian-style buildings painted in ochres and cin-namons, Wedgwood blues and honey-golds.

They drove beside the wide, curving Danube into Transdanubia where poppies coloured the hills red and the larks and swallows were so thick in the air that Suzanne could hear them above the drumming of the car and László's occasional and surprising bursts of singing.

He sang for joy, she thought in sudden surprise. Like the birds! Her eyes slanted over to look at his profile. It was contented. Happy... Devastatingly, dangerously attractive. And she knew that her mind was becoming captured by him, that he was dominating her world—and she was continually looking for the hints of warmth, vulnerability and humanity beneath the cunning face he presented. If she wasn't careful, he'd take her heart too. He had that kind of charisma.

He saw her looking and grinned. 'How about going south till the butter melts?'

She quelled the treacherous leap of her heart at the urge to say yes. 'You said we'd go to your office,' she answered primly.

'I did. Almost as good, I suppose. This is it.'

He turned off the road and drove straight towards a pair of elaborate gates, tooting his horn all the while. 'Ferenc!' he yelled, greeting the man who came running cheerfully from the small lodge house.

Curious, Suzanne noted Ferenc's delight and the eagerness with which he swung open the gates. If he talked to *her* like that, with that kind of affection, she mused, she'd become bound to him for ever. And would he be a brute to her, or a considerate lover?

She smiled wryly to herself. Fortunately she'd never know. Her thoughtful eyes watched the excited exchange between the two men then they clasped hands and László drove on.

'How long's he been with you?' she asked suddenly.

'About fifteen years.'

That made her frown. Employees stayed if they were content, well paid, well treated. Preoccupied with the knowledge, she realised that they were driving through flower meadows and ancient parkland.

'This is your office?' she asked suspiciously. 'It looks more like the private grounds of someone's house to me.'

'It's both,' he smiled, his voice velvet-soft with affection. 'It began life as the hunting lodge for the Knights of St John in the fourteenth century, then it was expanded for the Esterházy family four hundred years later. I use it as my office sometimes and for meetings. Terrible opportunists, the first Esterházys,' he confided. 'Married for convenience and wealth, changed sides in wars to suit their fortunes.'

'You must feel very much at home in an environment like that,' she said sourly. The house came into view; a small and unpretentious stone manor house with melon-coloured walls and a steeply tiled roof that seemed typical of the region. 'Wait a minute—you said you didn't have a home!' she accused. Her hands fidgeted in her lap. Homes meant privacy. Bedrooms.

'Relax,' he chuckled. 'I don't. This belongs to my daughter.'

'Your...daughter?' she said faintly, her head whipping around so fast that some of her wind-swept hair flew across her face.

'Sure.' Still a little way from the house, László stopped the car and leaned over, his fingers gently lifting the strands of hair from where they'd stuck on the cherry-red lipstick that glossed her mouth. His touch on her ear and the closeness of his warm face as he tucked the hair into the snood was electrifying. 'Does the idea that I'm a family man make you feel safe?' he murmured.

Safe, she thought breathlessly! Nowhere within ten miles of this man would be safe! 'Not at all,' she replied coolly. 'To be in the company of a lecherous——'

His mouth hit hers. Hard, demanding and driving her back against the seat, whisking away her breath and raising her blood-pressure far above the norm. Her moan of delight was hastily changed to a more ladylike protest but he was unstoppable, softening the kiss to a warm and distracting exploration that was more thorough than she could bear.

Kissed up a storm, she thought dreamily, all thoughts of revenge driven from her mind. Storm? Closer to a hurricane. The wild beat of her heart thudded against his shirt-front, mingling with his own alarmingly frenzied tattoo that made her breasts tighten with dreadful eagerness.

His arms enclosed her, holding their fluid, melding bodies, and nothing could prevent her hands from lifting to his hair, his beautiful, silken hair; curling wickedly at the nape of his neck, thick and strong at the temples... He was a father. Heaven help her, he had a child—a little daughter—who might be watching her daddy in horror even now! She had to escape.

But his mouth tugged and plundered hers, she didn't want to tear herself away and she was trapped, wasn't she?

Hating herself for her reluctance to elude his ardent caresses, she did what she had to for her own good and began to reach for the door-handle. It was a slow business, hampered by her desire to stay right where she was, enjoying the most sneaky and masterly arousal she'd ever known.

Snail-like in its speed, her hand stole away from his neck and slid down his shoulder. It was broad and muscular and for a moment the latent power of the flexing, shifting, flesh and bone filled her with a feminine thrill. Suzanne felt as though she were walking through a lake of warm water, all her movements indolent and languid, her mind and body willing him to caress her, to keep kissing her with that hard, fierce and irresistible mouth...

She gasped. His tongue touched the centre of her lips and they had parted for him with dreadful eagerness. 'Oh, László!' she mumbled in dismay. It felt sweet to taste. Moist, probing—please, please, she begged, waiting, waiting for its deep entry to her mouth. Without realising it, she pressed harder against him and increased the force of their mouths. No; she *had* realised what she was doing, but she didn't want to admit it because then she'd be honour-bound to stop.

But what chance did she have? she thought hazily, winding sinuous arms around him again, all plans of escape forgotten. Or, she sighed distractedly, all escape abandoned. His touch made her body leap, his mouth— she couldn't get enough of it, needed to feel ravished by his burning lips that scattered her senses to the four winds.

'Wonderful,' he murmured huskily. 'So wonderful...'

And then something went off in her head. Moulded to him, she became aware that he lay half across her and there was a fire between them that she couldn't quell. It raged through her body and his, making them clutch each other helplessly, gripping with their hands, roughly caressing muscle, bone, warm satin skin, their mouths now fighting for equal possession and tongues touching, sharing in the sensitisation and exquisite agony of the shockingly sexual kiss that rocked her to the core.

'Hold me, hold me!' she urged, as though the powerful male arms weren't enough. 'Tighter!' she breathed.

His weight bore her down. His leg straddled hers, the hard ridge of his hip giving her a welcome knowledge of his utterly male body. And she felt herself moving sensually beneath him, exulting in the deep throaty groan that emerged from his mouth and flowed into hers.

A shaking hand slid between them and tentatively enclosed her firm breast. With some shock, she realised it had become engorged and tipped with a puzzlingly hard, throbbing peak. Embarrassed, she sought to move his hand away, but he diverted her by sliding his mouth over her throat in greedy kisses—and then his thumb was edging across her nipple and she could do nothing but remain totally still and enjoy every sinful second as he rubbed to devastating effect and she moaned and gasped at the unendurable havoc that small, insignificant gesture created within her.

So many nerve-endings on her body... All screaming for the pressure of his powerful body, voracious hands, his persuasive mouth—and he seemed gloriously intent on satisfying her aching flesh, touching her as though he wanted to shape her body in his mind for ever.

'You are so lovely,' he whispered in awe and any remaining bones that she possessed seemed to melt at his husky cry. 'So responsive.'

Languorously she sighed, shaken by the lyrical sensation that was washing through every inch, every pore, every vein. 'I feel...' Her tongue clove to the roof of her mouth at the thickness of her own voice. She felt wanton. If there hadn't been a small voice of caution, if she hadn't been inexperienced and a vicar's daughter, if he weren't quite so accomplished a seducer, she would have gladly given way to the tearing hunger within her.

What they were doing didn't seem wrong, whatever her conscience was telling her. With this man, for the first time in her life, she was discovering how compelling a kiss could become. In his arms, fixed by his smouldering gaze, she'd temporarily lost all sense of reality. He had the ability to make her forget logic and fly like a bird, soaring into the endless blue and singing a wild song of joy.

Perhaps his passion came from his desire for love in any form. Perhaps hers stemmed from the irresistible combination of sexual hunger and tender compassion. The glimpses she'd had of the man beneath the ruthless steam-roller had touched her heart and it was unfolding beneath the fervour of his impassioned lips.

But. There was a big 'but'. Damn her logic! she whimpered. And was answered by László's muted growl, as his hands slipped beneath her crisp shirt and encountered warm, yielding flesh.

'Suzanne!' he breathed harshly.

Petrified by the shake in his voice, the knowledge that she had to do something now or she'd be stripped naked—in the car, in full view of the house!—she quickly slid her hand down the length of his beautiful, muscled arm, willed herself not to let it linger on the hand that was softly inciting her breast to swell against his palm, and found the hard chrome door-handle.

She took a deep breath, groaned at one wildly arousing initial squeeze of her nipple and, before she weakened with fatal result, she frantically jammed the heel of her hand downwards on the handle. The door swung open. She fell backwards and while László was reaching out to save her, she rolled away from under him and tumbled to the gravel drive.

'Damn! Are you all right?' he asked in concern.

Her hands splayed out, small pieces of grit embedded in her palms. Struggling to gain her feet, she was hampered by the slim skirt and László was pressing her back down to the ground again before she could get very far.

'*No*! I want to get up!' she complained. 'Oh, look at my stockings! Both laddered! Uhhhh!' Her voice shattered. He'd run his smooth hand down her leg and sent desire flooding upwards. 'And—and—my shoes!' she croaked, ashamed of the deep glow inside her. 'The— the leather's ruined! How can I look anywhere near decent and businesslike when I meet the bosses of the co-operatives if I'm——?'

László's laughing mouth enclosed hers for a briefly blissful moment and then he was patting her trembling hand, turning it over and carefully removing the grit from her flesh. 'Stop wittering on,' he chided with gentle mockery. 'Let's sort one thing out at a time. First, are you all right? Bruised anywhere?'

Her huge, melting eyes met his. Yes, she was bruised. Her lips. Her breasts. Her pride. But not inside. She was empty there, longing for him to always be gentle with her, to abandon his cruel revenge and . . . just to be her lover. She closed her eyes at the terrible admission she'd made to herself.

'My hip aches,' she said stiffly, refraining from telling him about the more painful ache that cried to be satisfied.

'I'll rub it in a moment——'

'No! I don't want you to touch me!' she yelled in panic, trying to scramble away. Eyeing him angrily, she saw triumph in his expression and her mobile, kiss-softened mouth tightened in rage. He thought she was a push-over! 'You're cutting into my schedule as it is!' she declared, hoping her single-mindedness would put him off.

'That's true. I think we'd better get you to your feet,' he said solemnly. 'And into the house.'

'What *will* your little girl think?' she groaned, as he tenderly placed his hands under her arms and brought her upright again.

'My...you mean my daughter?' His eyes were dark and veiled, as though he was hiding secrets again.

She ruefully examined her shoes. The soft kid leather was scratched, but nothing that a good polish couldn't cure. 'Of course,' she said absently, brushing her skirt. 'Something wrong?'

'*You* are wrong,' he said quietly. His voice hardened. 'My daughter is nearly as old as you. She's eighteen and is married with a three-month-old child.'

CHAPTER SEVEN

HER breath rasped in with shock. He was serious. 'I—
I can't believe it!' she said faintly, looking at him
askance. 'You're not even the marrying kind, let alone
a family man!'

'I never claimed that I sat at home and waved rattles,'
he pointed out drily.

'Oh, an absentee father, leaving all the work to the
little woman at home!' she scorned. 'That's just the kind
of thing a womanising renegade like you would do!'

'Shall we walk?' he drawled. 'It will ease your hip, I
think, and give you time to come to terms with the fact
that you've been kissing a grandfather.'

She scowled at the lurking dance of laughter in his
voice. 'I wasn't kissing anyone. You were.' Her hauteur
dissolved when she thought of the craziness of what
they'd just done. 'A grandfather!' she said in strangled
tones as they made their way down the drive. 'I've been
jumped on by someone's grandpa!' Her mouth twitched.
It was too ridiculous! Despite her anger, she couldn't
help grinning. She ought to be furious with him, but . . .
'A wrinkly! My god!'

Stunned, she examined him as he walked along beside
her, his arm securely around her waist. He was lithe and
sinuous, moving with the ease of a stalking panther, and
he had the taut-strung power of a young man—no, more:
there was a dynamic drive in everything he did that his
carefully assumed sardonic manner couldn't conceal. He
was more alive, more filled with energy than any guy
she'd ever known.

'You haven't got any wrinkles!' she accused wryly.

The lustrous dark eyes flicked in her direction. 'It must
be my pact with the Devil,' he grinned wickedly. 'Or the
constant application of a flat iron.'

She tried to stem a giggle but it surfaced. 'Brown paper and a trouser press,' she suggested.

'Absolutely,' he said, laughing. 'That and the steam roller.'

'A grandfather! This is crazy!' she said in bemused tones, shaking her head.

He stopped and turned her to him, his hands cradling her face. 'Isn't it?' he said huskily. 'I begin to teach you a lesson and find that you're teaching me one: that a kiss is the most risky action a man can ever take.' His eyes glittered and though his words were caressing, she sensed an element of forced sincerity that made her spine stiffen. 'Don't you have the feeling that there's something very special between us, Suzanne?'

'No,' she mumbled. 'It's illogical. You know it is. Everything's against our liking each other, let alone wanting to—to...' She gave up trying to elaborate. 'There must be a rational explanation,' she finished lamely.

His gently pitying smile softened his face. 'There never is anything rational about mutual attraction,' he murmured silkily. 'There's nothing you can do about the chemistry between two people. Perhaps we have to accept that and see where it leads us.'

She knew he was probably trying to seduce her for reasons of his own, far beyond desire. And yet she felt instinctively that he did feel more for her than pure animal lust. But then she couldn't trust her judgement any more. Even though she wanted to, very, very badly.

Suzanne lowered her eyes so that she didn't see the warm affection in his expression. She could take the sexual hunger. Affection was more difficult to cope with. And then she looked harder and beyond the smiling mask she saw that his eyes weren't friendly at all. They seemed remote and cold, as if he were suppressing some violent emotion. Trembling slightly, she wondered warily what he was up to now.

'We don't have to accept it at all. And of course we can do something about it,' she said stubbornly. 'We—we both had our own reasons why we wanted...' She blushed.

'To make love,' he said and in the honey of his voice she heard a yearning that foolishly she believed went beyond sex.

Love, she thought dreamily. To make love with this guy... She blushed, stopping her brain from presenting her with sensual images. 'No! I—I'd been through a lot. I needed someone to hold me. You happened to be the only one around. But... I'm not inviting sex!'

'Unfortunately, you are,' he murmured lazily, his eyes glittering like a ravenous tiger's.

'You keep your distance!' she said hotly. 'We're on opposite sides of the fence. You're blackmailing me to get what you want and it must be obvious that I despise you. You're miles older than I am and have a married daughter, for heaven's sake! We have to forget this nonsense——'

'Yes,' he agreed wryly, the expressive mouth firmly under control. 'Whatever possessed us?'

She felt confused. One minute he was all over her, the next he was dismissing the heated session as though it had meant nothing. Perhaps that was how he normally carried on, she thought gloomily. Women were probably ten-a-penny for him. He could take them or leave them, but probably wasn't prepared to fight madly for the privilege of possessing any particular one. So she shrugged her slender shoulders. 'Search me,' she said casually.

'It's an interesting suggestion but I'll pass for the moment. Come on,' he murmured, collecting her briefcase. 'Let's get you indoors and we'll see what can be done about your ravished appearance.'

'Oh! That bad?' she cried anxiously. Her crestfallen face lifted to his. 'I think I need to sit down,' she said plaintively, suddenly drained.

'Bit shaky, are you?' he enquired innocently.

She glared. 'From the fall.'

'Ah.'

He was laughing inside, she knew he was. Determined to regain her composure and dazzle him in a moment

with her intelligent analysis of her business plan, she remained stiff and aloof while he walked her slowly and
with the utmost care around the back of the house.

Donkeys and hardy all-weather ponies grazed in a
small paddock and a herd of geese came to greet them.
While László was shooing them away with good-natured
skill, she leant against a post and rail fence and felt the
slow, languid peace—despite the honking geese—fold
around her.

Swallows were weaving in and out of some thatched
barns and cats lay curled up in a painted cart, its shafts
entwined with bindweed. And beyond the ripening fruit
of an apple orchard she could see serried rows of vines
marching up a hill with nothing beyond but forest and
more hills, a misty smoke-grey in the heat haze.

'Some office!' she commented when he returned.

'Nothing better,' he agreed gravely. Stepping over a
duck he pushed a huge iron key into the plank door and
invited her in.

She expected his daughter to come running, but there
was a slumbering silence. And a kitchen of barn-like
proportions, warm, cosy and in more chaos than she
could ever have imagined possible.

'László! How awful for you! You've been burgled!'
she cried in horror, and caught his arm in genuine
sympathy.

He gave her a puzzled look, studied the scattered socks,
jumpers, shoes and T-shirts, checked over the bunches
of herbs all higgledy-piggledy on the big scrubbed pine
table and began to move cabbages and dark red cherries
from one of the chintz armchairs.

'Perhaps we have,' he grinned, sampling a plump
cherry with a connoiseur's enjoyment. 'Mmm. Perfect.
Burglary? We'd never know. It always looks like this.
Nice of you to care.' He smiled at her look of horror as
she gazed around. 'It's clean,' he assured her. 'Have a
seat and take off your stockings.'

She looked at the chair dubiously. With a sigh, László
clambered over the chaos on the floor with the ease of
a man used to such activities and reached up for a towel

hanging from a pair of antlers on the wall, ceremoniously placing it on the chintz cover.

'Thank you,' she said primly and sat down, determined to get over his revelations as fast as possible. She had business to do. 'Turn around,' she said stiffly. 'I'm not having you ogle my thighs when I peel off my stockings.'

'You're dreadfully buttoned up for such a young woman,' he mocked. 'You really ought to let go a little.'

She refrained from saying that she thought she had—and where had that led her? To a rapidly unbuttoned shirt! 'You're supposed to complain about the younger generation,' she said tartly, 'but not to deplore their high moral code.'

László's mouth quivered. He looked more like a powerful and hungry sex symbol, rather than a man with anything as carpet slipperish as a family. 'I'll find some things for lunch,' he said drily and opened a larder door.

While she fumbled surreptitiously with her suspenders, like a prude undressing on a cold British beach, she stared at the marble shelves of the huge cupboard in surprise. They were stacked floor to ceiling with jars of pickles and preserves, bottled fruit, jams, vinegars, oils... And hanging from the rafters were smoked hams and sides of bacon, black sausages and strings of onions and garlic, dried apple slices, peaches, apricots...

She beamed. It was beautifully rural and gave her a comforting feeling. Realising this was dangerous with László around, she quickly peeled down her stockings then rolled them up and put them in her bag. 'Who keeps house here?' she asked, enormously impressed by the air of industry.

'Whoever's around,' he said casually. 'All of us at times. When the fruit or vegetables are ready for picking we all set to and sit at the table slicing or blanching. It bonds us together, I think.'

'So you do stop to wave rattles sometimes.'

'Did I say that?' he hedged.

But she knew he did, and that he was protecting himself from her. A small part of her heart began to sing. He loved his family. It was an important point and she felt immediately warmer towards him.

'Your daughter isn't here?' she ventured a little nervously.

'I asked her to disappear for the day. But don't worry,' he drawled, seeing her look of alarm. 'I merely wanted us to be free from the Mother and Baby routine.'

He loved them. He couldn't keep the pride from his voice, however dismissive he tried to be. 'I'd be a fool not to worry, alone with you,' she muttered.

His dark eyes simmered, lighting fires within her again as easily as if he'd kindled tinder. 'We must both remember the purpose of our collaboration and keep that uppermost in our minds,' he said softly. 'There are things I want which take precedence over my loins.'

She gulped at his directness and avoided his gaze. 'I agree,' she muttered. 'We both want to make me successful. Me for praiseworthy reasons, you for vindictive ones.' Her eyes slanted to his and saw he was hastily hiding a smile. 'You have another reason for putting me in your power, don't you?' she asked quickly.

'Have I?' he drawled and she fumed with frustration. 'Go up to the bathroom if you think the sight of your bare legs will inflame me,' he said laconically. 'First on the right up the stairs. There'll be clean towels in the linen cupboard in there. Use any that aren't white—those are for the baby. You'll find some new stockings in the bedroom opposite. My daughter has a fetish for that luscious little gap of thigh at the top of her legs, like you.'

Suzanne felt the blush creep over her skin at his earthy mouth as he contemplated the smooth line of her thighs beneath her skirt. 'I couldn't possibly take anything of hers,' she began stiffly.

'So how are you going to look, marching into a textile mill in bare legs?' he enquired in a lazy drawl.

'Damn you!' she muttered. Why did he always have the last word—and why was it always perfectly rational? She couldn't even argue with him without appearing to be unreasonable.

'Can't logic be infuriating sometimes,' he observed.

Her eyes iced over. Wretched man! She decided not to rise to his bait. He liked nothing better than to fight. With his laughter ringing in her ears, she gingerly negotiated the obstacle course that covered the kitchen floor and padded out, shoes in hand, up the prettily painted stairway to a luxurious bathroom.

After washing her grazes, she made her way to the bedroom across the landing. Every available surface of the sunny room was filled with babywear, toys and photographs. And she couldn't stop herself from investigating. László's late wife would be in one of them, she was sure.

Her fascinated eyes scanned each lovingly displayed photo. Lots of László—obviously his daughter adored him. He must have waved rattles, she thought. She blinked. László and a dumpy, homely woman with a laughing face were holding a child each. Two children, then, both girls. There they were again, older; dark copies of their father but with their mother's twinkling eyes. And László himself looked as she'd never imagined possible: happy, contented, proud.

Busily revising her idea of his sophisticated, elegant wife, she didn't hear him come in till he spoke. 'Oh, dear,' came his slow drawl. 'You've discovered the menagerie.'

She whirled around and saw him in the doorway, as cynical as ever. It dawned on her that she'd expected to find him every inch the proud father, all tender affection and soft-eyed with memories. She must have been mad. When it suited him, László had gold for blood. And dollar signs pumping his heart.

'Menagerie! What a fond father you are!' she scathed. He merely pursed his mocking mouth, his eyes undressing her with their usual insolence. Unsteadily, she went to the dressing table and tried to dismiss his powerful masculinity from her mind. Carpet slippers, she told herself. Fatherhood. Nappies, rusks, sleepless nights...oh, God! she thought in horror, a vision of László in bed, making love to... 'Your second daughter…how old is she?' she asked, desperate to divert herself.

'Dinah's eighteen, as I told you; Lara is fifteen.'

'Do they know their father blackmails people?' she asked coldly, searching for some stockings. Anything to cover up the fact that she was trembling. László in a room was bad enough. In a bedroom, he was positively lethal.

'Blackmail? I've hardly begun. There's more to come,' he said with soft menace.

Hastily she backed up against the chest of drawers, her eyes wary of the sensual slick of his tongue over his lips as he contemplated her. He meant seduction! 'You wouldn't touch me here, with your family photographs all around!' she grated.

'There are plenty of other places. The stairs. The bath. The barns——'

She swallowed. 'You said we had a lot to discuss!' she hissed.

He leaned against the door-jamb, blocking her escape route and managing to look sexually threatening at the same time. 'More than you know,' he mused.

Pretending he didn't unnerve her, she deliberately turned her back on him and strode into the en-suite bathroom where she slammed and bolted the door, slipped on the stockings and emerged again quite cold and collected, pushing past him and his tension-making body. He didn't grab her as she'd feared. But she felt his exhalation of warm breath on her face and a turbulence rocketed through her body as though he'd assaulted her physically. Her breath caught in her throat and he heard that, because he chuckled in a sinister and arrogant way that had her balling her fists and wishing…

'Violent emotions,' he murmured in a velvety soft voice, 'are often the precursor to sex.'

'Or murder,' she croaked. And she wasn't sure herself what she really wanted to do: kiss him or kill him. Both, she thought miserably, stemming the surge of her wayward, treacherous desires. 'It's only the thought of your lovely money that's stopping me from knifing you in the back.'

'Mercenary little bitch,' he said amiably.

'Well-matched, aren't we?' she said with a proud tilt of her chin.

'A perfect fit,' he agreed. His husky drawl and the smoky blaze within his eyes tormented her starved body.

And, conscious of the danger, she gave a brief 'Huh!' and darted down the stairs to the safety of the kitchen.

He was used to this flirting; it must be second nature now, she reasoned, whereas she was quite hopeless at coping with lusting males. She had to remember that he was constantly trying to keep her under his thumb. Or his body. Either would suit him fine, she thought angrily.

Opening her briefcase, she sifted through the papers and arranged them neatly on the kitchen table in front of her, after pushing aside the plates of tempting food he'd placed there. 'Let's get to work,' she said frostily, when he appeared. With his jacket removed and shirtsleeves rolled up, he looked as though he was ready for business at last, she thought in relief. Small drops of water glistened on his forehead as though he'd doused his face. Good. He needed to cool down.

He smiled as if he knew how agitated she really felt. 'If you like. I'll kick off,' he suggested. 'There are one or two things I need to know. For instance, I want to get your aims clear,' he said, straddling a chair opposite her. 'Why choose to sell by mail order? What's wrong with retail?'

'I did a study,' she said firmly. 'Retail outlets aren't making money at the moment unless there's a chain of them, whereas home shopping's on the up and up. It's going to take off in a big way and I want to be there when it does.'

The piercing black eyes burrowed into hers. Strip off the sardonic, sexual predator, she mused, and you were left with the bones of a ruthless inquisitor.

'You're right,' he agreed surprisingly. 'We'll come to your supply problems later, but let's stick with your products. You say in your proposal that you want to feature Hungarian shirts. What else?'

She was about to tell him that she didn't expect to have the funds for items other than those close to home; perhaps Eire and Brittany. And then she remembered something he'd said about funds. Her eyes lit up. At long last she could turn the tables on him!

'Since this morning,' she said sweetly, 'I've expanded my horizons. Originally I'd thought to start small.' Her smile became broader. 'With your generous offer of funds, I can start big.'

'It's not going to be that generous,' he remonstrated, mildly amused by her self-assurance.

'On the contrary. You're going to be very generous. We agreed that you would have forty per cent of my profits in exchange for—and I quote,' she said with great relish, ' "unlimited funds". I intend to use those funds. Unlimited ones. I'll take what I want—unless you want to withdraw the agreement and settle for, say, ten per cent? Our conversation is on tape,' she reminded him smugly. 'Use it against me and it will confirm your rather rash remark.'

'Damn!' he said with mild self-reproach. Suzanne wondered why he wasn't horrified. He ought to be; it had been a stupid, boastful thing to say... Hadn't it? He sighed expansively and shook his head at her. 'It seems you've got me over a barrel,' he admitted. 'Tell me how you mean to spend my money.'

Too excited to stop and consider why he wasn't gnashing his teeth and tearing out his hair, she let the exhilaration well up inside her. Instead of holding back and going slowly towards her dream, she was all set for an accelerated ride!

'I'm going to India,' she said, elation edging into her voice. 'There'll be the opportunity to go into production with tunics and trousers there——'

'Watch them on delivery,' he cautioned calmly. 'They're wonderful on all fronts, but an understanding of time isn't their strongest point. And most countries with a recent Soviet past need watching for quality control. In the old days, customers were glad to get a shirt at all, let alone one that had the same buttons or the same collar every time.'

'Oh.' He seemed very knowledgeable. 'Thank you.' She tried to goad him into admitting he regretted his reckless remark about funds. 'I thought I'd go to China next,' she said slyly, 'for their silk pyjamas—and perhaps the work outfits,' she said, inventing on the spot. The world was her oyster. Anywhere, she could go anywhere!

'Slow down,' he drawled. 'You'll have a lot to contend with.' He smiled at a secret joke and she felt as if a cloud had crossed the sun. Trouble, she remembered; he had yet to tell her his final revenge.

'Aren't you annoyed that I'm going to spend your money so freely?' she asked. 'It could cost——'

'One pays for everything in the end.' He leaned forwards, his elbows on the table, the strong, tanned arms flexing before her appreciative eyes. 'You have plans. You want me to help you realise them——'

'Ye-e-es,' she said doubtfully, not pinning her hopes on any rainbow he might choose to create. 'I have a ten-year proposal. Why?'

He shrugged and grinned lazily. 'The more I am responsible for fulfilling your dreams, the more it annoys István. Petty, isn't it?' he murmured.

'Yes.' Her eyes were thoughtful. It sounded small-minded but she knew full well there was more to it than that. Something very important indeed was causing László to deliberately pour money into her venture. Or to pretend to, she thought, chewing over that possibility and making a mental note to tie him down legally till the red tape strangled him.

She felt sure that he hadn't made a mistake about offering her unlimited funds because he hadn't batted an eyelid when she'd slyly proposed her world tour. It was possible that he'd deliberately planted that remark to see if she made use of it. Did that make her an opportunist, like him? Or... was he steering her into deceptively safe waters before he sank her ship?

'Next question,' he said smoothly, bringing her mind back again. 'How long from sample to production?'

'Nine months.' Her eyes narrowed. He was flicking through a photostat of her analysis, one he must have acquired by subterfuge. 'How did you get hold of that?' she asked indignantly.

'I'm very sneaky,' he told her—as if she didn't realise that! 'I persuaded a pretty secretary to get copies for me. Lovely girl. Ate like a horse, drank like a fish.'

'Nasty methods,' she said primly.

'That's what she said,' he admitted, his sensual mouth curling as if with pleasant memories. Probably of enforced sex, she thought with distaste. 'Why a hundred-page brochure?'

Suzanne gave a small frown of annoyance and searched for the relevant section in her proposal. He'd seduce anyone to get what he wanted. Her hands suddenly trembled. Seducing her would be another joke—something else to flaunt in István's face. Her loins tightened. She'd been very silly to imagine that László's interest had been a purely healthy, man-woman response, or even a bargaining point to acquire a percentage of her profit.

'I investigated other firms,' she said, coldly efficient. 'It seems to be the best length on balance. I've plenty of market research on that if you want to see it. Later I plan to establish a children's section and perhaps add linen as well. For now, I want to concentrate on adult wear.'

'Sounds limiting. Not sure I agree. How do you intend to handle the problem of copying traditional designs?' he frowned.

She kept her head and didn't argue. 'By taking the best of each style and keeping the essence of it—but I'll create my own special details and use more commercially viable fabrics.' She leaned forward earnestly, trying to treat this like an ordinary proposal. He was nothing but a banker to her. She giggled to herself. In carpet slippers. 'The most difficult part,' she said, trying to hold down her amusement, 'will be the selection. There'll be dozens of ideas I could use, but I have to get a balanced choice. And I must decide what'll appeal to the customer's love of the past but make it wearable too. What do you think of producing felt capes, the ones the shepherds here have made for centuries?'

'They won't sell,' he said firmly.

Crushed, she thought again. 'But waistcoats would. Frogged, with a little traditional felt appliqué——'

'Perhaps. Talking of tradition, there's a mayor of a small town who prints indigo fabric by hand in his spare time,' László said thoughtfully. 'You can only buy the fabric between May and September, because that's when he hangs it outside to dry.'

'Wonderful story!' she cried, unable to keep her expression indifferent. She'd had an idea. 'I could sell Hungarian shirts in white or indigo—and put that story in the brochure. In fact, each item could have an anecdote, or a sentence or two about its history.'

'Customer involvement...' he mused. 'I'll tell you this. Passing on information about the culture of each country will endear you to your outworkers—and the authorities who give you the permissions. You'll be bound to get more co-operation from everyone involved. They'll be flattered that their traditions are valued. Inspirational, Suzanne.' He grinned. It was the grin of a starving tiger and she sighed, realising that he didn't praise her for nothing. 'Let's drink to it.' But all he did was reach for a bottle and pour her a glass. 'To our success,' he said softly. 'I'm looking forward to this afternoon immensely.'

So was she. Thrilled, Suzanne downed the wine and helped herself to some slices of fresh gammon. Her head was whirling with the excitement of it all and it was difficult to keep calm. 'I can't wait to begin. I've worked so hard for this!' she exclaimed, hardly daring to believe that everything she'd wanted was coming her way.

'So have I.'

Her eyes flicked up at the fervour in his voice. And then it occurred to her that he needed her to succeed—if only to annoy István. Therefore, with his support, she would. István and Tanya would remain in blissful ignorance that they had no right to their inheritance and life would be full of fascinating journeys, meetings, and joyful homecomings to Widecombe and her own warehouse.

'You have stars in your eyes,' said László huskily.

She took a more cautious sip of wine. 'I have the sun and the moon and all the planets,' she replied wryly. 'Thanks for your input—financial and otherwise. I know you have unpleasant reasons for helping me, but I am delighted, nevertheless. I would have achieved my ambition on my own, of course,' she added quickly, 'but you're getting me there faster.'

He lifted his glass and smiled at her over its rim. 'To a remarkable woman,' he murmured. 'To success, to our dreams.'

She drank. Then, to make sure her head didn't spin, she ate heartily. And after, they took their coffee outside in the sunshine with the ducks and hens running beneath their feet and she wondered if she'd ever been so happy in the whole of her life.

'We ought to be making a move,' she sighed, reluctant to leave the tranquil, homely garden. 'We can't keep people hanging around at the co-operatives.'

László finished his liqueur and motioned for her to do the same. Then, when she made to rise, he stayed her with his hand. 'We're not going anywhere,' he said softly. 'We can't.'

Suzanne flung off his hand and scrambled to her feet. 'Oh, yes, we can!' she said a little wearily. 'Don't spoil this with your tricks——'

'No tricks,' he said laconically. 'It's the law of the land.' His mouth curved into a demonic smile of triumph. 'We've been drinking. Don't you know the percentage of alcohol allowed in your blood if you're driving in Hungary?'

'No,' she scowled.

'Nil.'

'Nil?' she repeated in dismay. Angrily she clenched her hands. 'You knew! You didn't stop me! You...oh!' she cried, stamping her foot in frustrated temper. Her plans had been ruined! 'How long?' she demanded. 'How long do you think before you can drive?'

He sucked in his breath dubiously. 'I should say... tomorrow morning,' he murmured. And slanted his wicked black eyes at her. Suzanne shrank back. Tomorrow. He licked his lips. 'I think we can fill our evening, though, don't you?' he purred.

She blanched. Judging by the calculating expression on his predatory face, he expected her to provide the programme of entertainment. She was a virtual prisoner in an isolated house, with only his word that his daughter was returning. Her smart shoes wouldn't take her far if she decided to make a run for it—and in any case, he was swifter and would bring her to the ground before she reached the nearest trees. She thought of the coming darkness, the fight she'd have to put up to keep him at arm's length, and knew she'd never succeed in resisting.

'I hate you!' she muttered miserably. He'd finally trapped her—and this time she feared there would be no escape. 'You planned this very carefully, didn't you?' she said coldly. 'As you plan every single action you ever take.'

'Don't you just admire my organisational abilities?' he murmured, and tilted his chair back till it was balancing precariously on two legs.

'You bastard! You've ruined everything I set up!' she cried furiously. 'What are we going to do about the appointments we had today—*if* you even bothered!' she accused.

'I am not, I have, cancel them and yes I did.'

He could hardly hold back the mocking laughter. Her scornful gaze swept up and down his arrogantly relaxed body. One heave and he'd be flat on his back, she thought maliciously. Tight-lipped, she glowered for a moment or two at his amused expression.

'I should lay you out in the dirt where you belong,' she snapped, hardly able to control the wild flame of temper licking through her. 'But I'll think of something better to make you regret your mean-minded manipulation!'

'Thought you didn't approve of revenge?' he murmured, pouring himself more coffee.

'This would be entirely justified,' she said coldly.

'But my dear Suzanne, that's precisely what all avengers believe,' he replied, his voice as soft as the breeze. 'Justice is the only thing that drives them.'

Dispirited, she lifted her face up to the perfumes that assailed her. Close by, an exuberant planting of herbs tumbled over the path and terrace, fragrant thyme and basil, lemon mint and marjoram seeding themselves with abandon in the cracks between the old stone slabs. The hot afternoon had drawn out the oils and filled the air with heady riches that mingled with the sweet Turkish coffee and László's Russian brandy. Which she glared at resentfully.

'It was so lovely here and you've ruined my stay,' she grated, her eyes hard, green-flecked slits. 'A friendly, cosy house, an idyllic garden——'

'Marjoram chicken, a loaf of bread, too much wine and me, my love in the Wilderness.'

Suzanne drew in a long, controlling breath. 'Look, Omar Khayyám——'

'Fitzgerald, actually,' he corrected blandly.

'Whoever,' she said through her teeth. 'I'm not your "love", I'm your business partner—and I'm regretting that——'

'I made sure we both drank too much to drive anywhere this afternoon. But my intention was not primarily seduction.'

'Oh, really,' she said sarcastically, driven beyond her usual sweetness. 'Enlighten me. Was it because you have shares in some plum brandy co-operative in Russia that we finished that bottle? You thought I needed an afternoon off? Or,' she suggested in acid tones, 'you thought it would be nice if we fed the ducks this evening?'

'Right on all counts,' he drawled. 'But mainly because I decided that it would be a good idea if you met my family.'

'I *beg* your pardon?' she said coldly.

László's mouth softened into a smile. 'The more I think about it, the wiser I realise I am. They'll be here shortly. Baby buggy, powdered milk, nappy-clad little dimpled bottom and all.'

His eyes flickered beneath the luxuriant fringe of black lashes and he lazily undid another shirt button. Suzanne was mesmerised by the glow of the late sun on the beautiful undulations of his chest and wondered frantically why she couldn't reconcile herself to the fact that he was a family man. All she saw was his lethal male power that crept into her body with insidious skill and made quite unfair demands.

Her hand flew to her mouth. He was staring at it with an earthy speculation and her instinct was to hide the fact that her lips had parted and flowered as if begging to be kissed. 'I'm sure it will be very nice for me to meet your family,' she said, her voice hopelessly husky. It was the relief, she told herself darkly. She'd imagined he'd be chasing her around the table and instead he'd be presiding at its head while they all talked about nappy rash.

'I hope so,' he said smoothly. 'And of course, you realise that I can't have planned to seduce you if I was expecting my family to turn up.'

She was struck dumb. Part of her was thanking her lucky stars. Part... She wriggled, uncomfortable with a wicked and wanton version of herself visualising the two of them sitting outside, through a long, drowsy afternoon and kissing till the sun set.

Feeling distinctly disconcerted, she settled back in her chair. An apology was due, but it stuck in her craw. 'If what you're saying is true,' she said defensively.

'Why shouldn't they? Dinah lives here. She has to bring Nikki back for his bath,' said László laconically. 'You're wondering, perhaps, why I should want you to observe me amid such domestic scenes. It's simple. I don't want our relationship to develop.'

She eyed him uncertainly. His voice was soft, but there was a steely core to it and when she met his level gaze she saw that he was quite serious, however startling his remark might be. 'You could have fooled me,' she said sourly.

'I'm sure I could,' he said sardonically. 'I've managed up to now. Look, I'm very attracted to you,' he said, very matter-of-fact, when she bristled with indignation. 'You're highly attracted to me—no, don't bother to deny it,' he told her, when she opened her mouth in an automatic protest. 'We can't pretend, either of us. I've made a pass or two at you and you've tried to do the decent thing and resist. But your heart was never in it. That made it difficult for me.'

'I'm so sorry!' she said, tartly sarcastic. His assessment of her willingness was mortifying. He read her mind too well.

'So am I,' he agreed wryly. 'You see, the truth is, that I don't want any women in my life——'

'And I don't want any men in mine! I can assure you that you won't be pestered by me!' she cried, piqued because he'd said that first. 'I'm not the sort to simper and cling just because you've kissed me——'

'Suzanne,' he said huskily, stilling her with his eyes, 'I'm not the sort to let a woman get under my skin just because I've kissed her, either. But we're going to be spending a good deal of time together if I'm to aggravate István to my complete satisfaction and if...' He clamped his mouth shut as if changing his mind about telling her something. 'I want our business relationship to be remarked upon,' he said, paying great attention to some cat hairs on his knee. 'I want it publicised, gossiped about.'

'You really are determined to rub it in, aren't you?' she muttered resentfully.

'There'd be no point otherwise. Even at its most basic, we'll be meeting to discuss strategy. And certainly to begin with you'll need me to put in a good word for you with the co-operatives, various suppliers of material, thread and buttons, to sit in on talks with managers and thrash out the requirements for the first samples. We'll be thrown into each other's company on long journeys, late at night, when we're both tired——'

He'd do all that for her. Why, why, why? she asked herself. 'You don't have to run by my side every time I go anywhere,' she muttered.

'I can afford a week of my time to see that you meet the right people,' he said, his face impassive. 'I'll level with you. I have an interest in promoting the image of women in Hungary—in creating role models as an example to others. Don't ask why. You don't need to know,' he said, when she tried to interrupt. 'For the moment, all you need to take on board is the fact that we'll be together more than is perhaps wise.'

'So?' she said belligerently. But her pulses were racing and inside she was secretly thinking that she'd never survive such intimacy. The desires that smouldered between them would be fanned into an inferno. The more she was with him, the more she felt drawn to him and her need to be touched by him was frightening. She'd have to break the invisible threads that pulled them together or she'd be in terrible trouble.

'Wise up, Suzanne,' he said quietly. 'Neither of us wants involvement. And yet . . .' He gave a mildly exasperated shrug. 'I lust after you.' His velvet eyes held her immobile. He did want her! she thought in a terrifying exultation before she could stop herself. And the flare of excitement in her eyes made his gaze soften to an erotic warmth while she groaned in despair at her wayward sexual nature. 'You're far too transparent for your own good,' he said with a frown. 'A weakening of my resolve is something I won't tolerate. I'd risk a clash of loyalties. Now you, with your keen logic, must see that we have two courses of action.'

'We do?' She folded her arms because somehow she had to stop her appalling habit of trembling every time he talked in that honey-sliding voice about his desire for her. She was weak to fall for his flattery—and that was all it was. László was so full of animal urges that he'd be aroused by anyone. She wasn't anyone special. Calmed by her logic, she lifted a querying eyebrow and felt pleased at her coolness under pressure.

'You want me to spell it out?' he said in mild exasperation. 'It's perfectly simple. Either we succumb to our natural urges and accept that's all it is—sex, pure and simple—or we find a way to kill our desire. Me, surrounded by nappies, seemed a fair attempt at doing that.'

'I'd only ever make love with someone I do love,' she said hotly, 'and never with a primitive animal who sees all women as a means to satisfying his insatiable appetite!'

'I take it that's a no,' he said sardonically.

'Of course! You're my enemy—the man who's divided me from my family. That's almost the worst thing you could do to me, you know. I never realised it before,' she said in dawning understanding. 'They've always been there, albeit in the background, supporting me, acting as friends, laughing, protecting me...' She turned to him angrily, her emotions riding high. 'If I lost the affection of my family permanently because of my alliance with you, I'd—I'd...'

She couldn't continue. Tears filled her eyes and the emotion blocked her throat. She loved them more than she could ever have imagined. They were all-important— and László could tear her away from them! She stared at him in horror through a blur of tears. By allying herself with László, she was jeopardising everything she loved; her family. She'd made a mistake, a terrible mistake—and it might be too late to draw back.

CHAPTER EIGHT

'So,' HE said softly. 'We get to the truth. You'd do anything to protect them, wouldn't you?'

'Well, I—I——' She gulped. She was giving him an insight into ways in which he could threaten her.

He leaned across the table, fixing her with his terrible eyes, struggling with fierce emotions. He gave a shudder of intense passion and then his eyes blazed. '*I want you!*' he breathed, like a driven man.

The instant explosion inside her caught her unawares. In a brief split-second he'd risen and taken her in his arms, hauling her to him roughly and fiercely kissing her tortured throat till she was too dizzy to do anything else other than cling and moan and enjoy.

I want him too, she thought, somewhere in the back of her drugged mind. More than he knows. But I want everything. I want to make him whole, to kill his desperation for revenge, to find the good man beneath the bad. I want... She shuddered, the scorch of his branding mouth too sweet and brief now to bear.

'Please, László!' she moaned, forcing herself to protest as he tenderly sipped her tears and made her heart lurch with unwanted longing.

'Damn you!' he muttered. 'I think I must play my ace.'

It had come. Gritting her teeth, she dashed her hand across her eyes and gave him a scornful look, her eyes bright, her mouth sullen with protest. 'Get it over with, then!' she challenged, lifting her chin rebelliously.

'What cards do I hold?' he husked into the dark recesses of her mouth. 'Mmm?' His tongue darted to torment her.

'Enough,' she muttered miserably, feeling the echoing dart of a thousand swords stabbing her heart.

129

'I thought so.' His tongue found her ear, his hands stroked, plundered, teased. Suzanne drew in a shocked gasp as curls of pleasure rolled through her defenceless body. Wonderful, she thought. Never stop. 'You see, Suzanne,' he said softly, 'I want to announce to your family that we're intending to marry.'

In his arms, she froze, all sensation suspended. Perhaps he continued to kiss her, to assault her body with his insolent hands. She didn't know. Only that she shook with anger and misery that he should destroy all her growing feelings for him by making a mockery of something so important.

He pushed her away, panting heavily in her ear, his hair dishevelled and he looked so utterly appealing that she couldn't prevent her treacherous heart from filling with misguided love.

'You bastard!' she said coldly, shaking so much that he had to catch her hands to steady her.

'Sit down!' he ordered. 'You'll stay here till you agree to say that you'll marry me. If you don't agree, I'll keep you here anyway and tell your family the news myself.'

She sat down. 'I can't believe you're saying this! You must have a reason,' she croaked bitterly. Didn't he always?

'Of course.' The black lashes swept down to his cheeks. 'I've established our...friendship in István and Vigadó's minds,' he said softly. 'Now they'll be prepared for the next step—and dreading it. Our engagement.' He leaned forwards, kissing-close, his damnably erotic mouth smiling with anticipation. 'I'll be able to threaten Vigadó with the prospect of our marriage if he doesn't agree to my terms for the vital deal I told you about.'

'I won't agree to marry you!' she stormed. 'I can't put them through that——'

'You have to,' he growled. 'Or you'll never see any of them again.'

'What...what do you mean?' she asked hoarsely.

If any other man had said that she would have laughed. But he was deadly serious. 'Just that,' he said with soft savagery. 'You will agree to marry me, or I'll release such hell into their lives and yours that you'll wonder what kind of devil spawned me.'

She felt faint. But she couldn't falter, *mustn't* show weakness. 'But the suggestion of marriage is absurd!' she said, through pale and feebly moving lips. 'They'll never buy such an idea——'

'Oh, they will,' he drawled. 'I'm considered quite a catch by mercenary women. And they know how determined you are to blaze a trail across Europe. And the world,' he added sardonically.

'*No!*'

'Then I must personally telephone István at his honeymoon hotel and give him the glad news,' he murmured. 'That'll spoil his lovemaking.'

'No!' she moaned. 'Why are you doing this? It's—it's too drastic a step——' she began in a small, fragile voice.

His eyes darkened with pain. 'It's a drastic situation,' he growled softly. Lines of strain marred the smoothness of his mouth. He was under great pressure, she thought in agitation. As much as she...

'But... to pretend we're—we're going to marry!' she protested. 'You're joking—it's not necessary...'

'I'd tie you up and strap you to the altar and kidnap a priest if I had to,' he said in a hard tone. 'Anything.'

'You're crazy!'

'No. Driven,' he corrected, and in the sweep of his hand through his hair she saw a man harrowed and racked by something far worse than envy or resentment.

'You must tell me why,' she whispered. 'I can see it's something vital to your happiness——' She tried again, shaken by the tremor in her croaking voice. 'You've got to understand what my family means to me!' she cried, her voice shaking with the intensity of her feelings. 'My business is terribly important to me because I've invested so much of my hopes and my life in it. But it isn't *that* important. I value the people I love far more. Keeping your existence from the countess and István isn't worth the break-up of our family—so take care how far you push me! I really took them for granted up to now,' she marvelled. 'But because you forced me to create a rift between us, I've discovered how much I love them, how much I need them all—and I'm sure they'd feel the same if I had to tell you to do your damnedest. Tanya would, I know. She's always put us first.'

'Perhaps I did you a favour.' His expression was unreadable. 'Families should never be taken for granted. In the end, they're all you have.'

Her tearful eyes searched his and she thought she detected compassion. Suddenly she wondered whether it might be an idea to tell him about her sisters and István's harrowing childhood. Maybe if she did, if he saw her family as people instead of enemies, he'd relent, talk to István and come to some mutual arrangement. He might even forget about avenging the past.

'You're right!' she said passionately, her voice breaking up a little. 'And you only learn to value something when you're in danger of losing it. I know my sister Mariann would be devastated if she knew I was hurting Tanya. She and Vigadó——'

'I don't want to hear about the bastard,' he said coldly, his eyes like slivers of black ice.

Wrong choice. She thought rapidly. He'd loved his father... Her face grew anxious when she thought how the abrupt announcement of her engagement to István's rival would agitate her own father.

'Have some compassion, László. My father's been ill,' she said huskily. 'We've kept our problems from him because he's had enough to contend with in his life. He'd be worried, upset...' Nothing had changed in László's harsh face. 'He was a vicar,' she went on tremulously. 'A good man. When Mother came over from Hungary as a refugee, destitute, stateless, he took her in and gave her work. They fell in love and were happy together. You can't hurt him. He's my father and I love him as much as you loved your father. Losing Mother devastated him.' She lifted her chin and shot straight from the shoulder. 'Still, you'd understand how traumatic it is to lose a lifetime partner, wouldn't you?'

'Don't push me,' he muttered, his eyes glittering. But his mouth had shown his raw pain and she knew she was hitting home.

'István was spirited from his birthplace like you,' she went on relentlessly. 'But he was less fortunate. He had a lonely and unhappy childhood. None of us knew that Mother had promised to teach him about his Hungarian traditions, or that she deliberately prevented him from becoming fond of us—can you imagine that?' she cried indignantly.

'I don't want to know!' he growled.

'No, because he's so similar to you!' she retaliated. 'In the wrong place, at the wrong time, wanting something he couldn't have: the love of his mother, her arms around him——'

'Shut up!' he rasped.

Suzanne steeled her heart to the choking emotion in his voice. She had to continue. She must break the circle of hatred and mistrust. He and István were half-brothers. They should be bonded together, not tearing each other apart.

'You think he had everything,' she said softly, her huge eyes filmy with tears. 'But he also bore our resentment because we didn't understand why every last penny was spent in educating him to be a gentleman——'

'Whereas I should have been the one to study estate management, the intricacies of the Hungarian language and the correct way to eat artichokes,' László muttered bitterly.

She winced. 'It's not our fault that you've been deprived of your birthright,' she muttered. 'And you don't *want* it, anyway! I don't understand——'

'You will, in time,' he said curtly. 'You'll discover what's important to me——'

'Some stupid business deal!' she taunted.

Suzanne's mouth set in a mutinous line, hating the way he treated her—as if she were a child, only to be told certain things. But she knew she couldn't afford to let her resentment colour her feelings. She must continue to break down the barriers he'd erected against her family. If he knew how sweet Tanya was, he'd never want to hurt her.

Flicking her eyes up to his, however, she saw that she was wrong. There was a glacial light in his eyes and a chilling expression on his face. He wanted something so badly that he'd sweep everything aside to get it. Her mind sought a way out. All she could do was to soften him up a bit. And suddenly she knew how. And changed tack, discovering that she could be as ruthless as he when the occasion warranted it.

'I'm sorry,' she said quietly. 'You've obviously got your reasons. It...it must have been difficult for you when your wife died,' she probed gently.

The dark eyes grew even icier. 'If you imagine I'm going to relent in my treatment of you just because you mention my late wife in sympathetic tones, you're mistaken,' he growled.

'You did love her.'

'Yes.'

'You weren't wearing a ring when I first met you,' she pointed out gently.

He frowned. 'Deliberately, so you weren't put off. It's a measure of my determination that I removed one of my few possessions I cherish,' he said harshly. 'So you can see that any attempt to soften me up by talking about my late wife will fail.'

'I was comparing her death to my own situation,' she said with quiet firmness. 'And how Tanya comforted Mariann and me when Mum died and made us feel we had someone to cuddle us and be our new mother. It was she who made us brave and helped us to think how much worse it was for Father who'd loved Mother so.' László began to gather the glasses and bottles noisily but she knew he was listening. 'Did your daughter help her sister to come to terms with the situation—and to see how much you were hurting—when your wife died, do you think?'

'Probably,' he jerked out.

The tenseness of his jaw was encouraging. 'It was hard for Tanya, as it must have been hard for your Dinah,'

she said shakily, aching for him and finding it difficult
to stay on course. 'I never knew all the sacrifices Tanya
must have made, but she put aside her own needs and
selflessly tended to ours. She's a wonderful woman,
László.'

'You do what you have to at times of stress,' he muttered. 'You rise to the needs of the moment.' The tray
remained on the table and he stared down at it as though
reliving old and painful memories.

Her heart went out to him. Whatever he was, he'd
suffered the loss of his wife and had struggled to raise
his children whilst juggling with the age-old problem of
securing their future. Life had been hard. He'd learnt
to fight and didn't know when to stop. Perhaps she could
help. She dearly, dearly wanted to.

To her surprise and his, her hand stole across the table
and came to rest on his. Then she lifted her compassionate face to his grieving mouth and the anguished
eyes and knew she could make some impact on his
emotions.

'You've suffered your share of grief,' she said huskily.
'So has my family. It's been a rough ride. Tanya—and
István—have fought hard for their happiness.' Her gentle
gaze willed him to acknowledge that fact. 'This is the
first time either of them has done anything for their own
pleasure. And now she's on her honeymoon——'

'And I'm sure that István's behaviour must be giving
her cause for distress,' said László quietly.

Suzanne bit her lip. 'Oh, God! What have you done,
László? If he's preoccupied or moody, she'll think there's
something wrong with her marriage!'

The remote eyes wavered briefly. 'Then he must reassure her.'

'But to do that, he'd have to tell her that it's me he's
worried about and she'll *still* be upset!' she argued miserably. 'She virtually became my mother. She still feels
responsible for me——'

'You're old enough and mature enough to take care
of yourself,' he said shortly.

'Oh, László!' she cried brokenly. Slowly his eyes swivelled to hers and she flinched at the pain there. But even through her misery, she felt hope. His reaction meant he could feel and respond to emotion. 'My sister, my dear sister who sacrificed herself to us and gave me so much, is probably crying right now because she thinks I've flung her love back in her face,' she said huskily. 'She'll be thinking that I'm so selfish and ambitious that I'm prepared to work with her husband's enemy against his express wishes! I can't bear that! Oh, can't you see, it's slicing me in two!'

'Suzanne, please——' he said hoarsely.

Her mouth trembled, the tears half-blinding her, but through the haze she could make out his strained features and forced herself on. 'Put your elder daughter in Tanya's position,' she pleaded. 'She must have taken on the role of mother. You'll know how that would have put responsibility on her shoulders and changed her from a carefree teenager into a woman overnight, that she must have bitten back her own grief for the sake of the rest of you——'

'Suzanne!' he said through his teeth. And could evidently say no more. Beneath her palm, his hand was shaking as he drew it away. He sat down heavily and poured himself a drink, knocking it back in one go. 'Hell!' he muttered.

There was a chance, she thought. She'd found his vulnerable spot. His family. Summoning up all her willpower, she took a deep inhalation of breath. 'I admire your daughter, as I admire anyone who copes with grief, because first you have to feel grief—and that means you care,' she said fervently. Her heart was in her mouth. She was almost there, she was sure. He'd spilt some of the brandy—and, oh, God! she thought, she wanted to hold him, and stroke his furrowed brow! 'So tell me something,' she said in a low tone. 'Would you want anyone to hurt your daughter now, after the distress she's suffered in the past?'

To her astonishment and confusion, László's expression had hardened. 'No,' he growled. 'I would protect my family against anyone. Anything!' he declared vehemently. 'The worst thing anyone can do to a man is to hurt his children.'

'Then you understand!' she said, puzzled even in her relief. 'You must have some comprehension of the hurt that comes when families are divided.'

'Oh, yes,' he said bitterly.

'You're forcing me to become an outcast. How do you imagine I feel? How do you think you'd feel if——?'

'Shut up!' he snarled irritably. Temper, she thought, her body as taut as a wire. She was getting to him. She *knew* reason would win in the end. 'Unlike you, I have no choice at all in what I have to do,' he said, his eyes pinpoints of pain.

'There's always a choice!' she cried in despair. 'Can't you see that what you're doing to me is a denial of your love for your own children?'

'No!' he roared, exploding at last. In a sudden movement that had his chair crashing to the floor, he came to his feet and stormed straight over the objects lying in his path. Apprehensively she watched till he was halted in his tracks by the barrier of the window. He stood glowering at the undulating hills but she knew he saw nothing because he was concentrating on containing some terrible, simmering hatred that was making his shoulders heave with passion. 'I love them, damn you! Them—not you, your sister, or your precious brother-in-law! My children are all I have that's important in this world. All I trust. Nothing, no one is closer to me. And no one will ever come between us or hurt them as long as I draw breath!'

'But that's precisely what I feel!' she raged. Her hand banged down on the table and then she had jumped up, striding quickly over to confront him, her hands on her hips in challenge. 'Think about what you're doing to us! We're your family, whether you like it or not! Tanya has married your half-brother. He has your blood! You must feel some tie between us——'

'None!' he snarled savagely. 'None at all!'

She rocked with his vehemence. Fear closed up her throat. The way he was looking at her was making the muscles in her stomach contract. Somehow she dredged up some courage. Her pride wouldn't let him bully her into turning tail and whimpering in a corner.

'You bastard!' she scorned. 'You're using me in the vilest way you can for some measly *deal* you want to make! It can't be that important that you have to abandon all decency to realise it. You're rich. You don't need the money. You're powerful; you don't need any more admirers to stroke your ego, massive though it is!'

'Careful,' he warned grimly.

'I'll take the risk,' she said coldly. 'If this deal is some exciting gamble, then you could get your kicks some other way. Leaping out of a plane without a parachute, for instance,' she suggested bitterly.

'I have to do this deal,' he said tightly. 'You will agree to marry me. And if you talk for a week, a month, a year, I will not be swayed by your emotional appeals.'

'Tell me what it entails and why it's so important,' she demanded. 'Make me understand. I'm prepared to make a rational judgement, based on the evidence you give me. Let me decide if it's important enough to carry out this charade.'

'You must be crazy!' he scathed, his mouth grim. 'I can't possibly tell anyone!'

'Because it's just some selfish whim of yours,' she said contemptuously. 'Some nasty act of revenge!'

'I wish it were! Don't taunt me. I will make you regret it. You're playing with fire, Suzanne!' he hissed.

'I know!' she wailed. 'But every time I think of Tanya and how her honeymoon is being ruined, it breaks my heart! Are you a sadist? Are you enjoying what you're doing to me?'

'No.'

'Oh, God! Then why do it?' she yelled.

Black, fathomless eyes slanted to hers. 'Because it will blow my world apart if I don't.'

Her groan welled up from the depths of her body. She'd failed. He wouldn't budge from his determination to dangle her in front of István's eyes like some torture instrument. Tanya—and then her father, Mariann, John, Lisa...the countess—all would believe that she'd wilfully chosen to side with László for her own selfish ends. They'd think she'd betrayed them for a pot of gold. Her father would think so too—and that she'd rejected all his teaching about morality. And László was perfectly prepared to put her through hell for his own ends.

'I have to get away from you,' she muttered through bloodless lips. 'I can't stay here. If I do, I won't be responsible for my actions——'

'You're staying!' he snarled.

'I'll escape!' she muttered.

'You can't drive my car. I've hidden the keys. There's no other transport,' he said shortly.

Her eyes widened. 'Ferenc—the man at the gate——'

'He can't drive. There are no neighbours. You're stuck with me. With your decision,' he said, his eyes glittering.

'Then point me at the telephone directory!' she grated. 'I'll hire a car.'

'You'll meet my family. And I'll use you for the purposes I wish.'

Her eyes searched his in frustration. Again, she found herself baffled. What was so all-fired important? Pride? She gave a groan of total defeat. She didn't understand. He remained an enigma. Slowly she began to walk across the terrace towards the kitchen door, her feet bruising the sweet herbs. Her mind sought an explanation because there always was one.

By the tangled honeysuckle, she paused, concentrating on going over the facts. He'd admitted that he was attracted to her. He'd engineered this meeting with his family so that she'd see him as a father, rather than a potential sexual partner. He saw a relationship with her as a threat. He was afraid of it—and almost certainly that was because he could never continue to use her with a degree of cruelty if the balance of their relationship changed to...to something close and warm and loving.

Her head lifted at an awful thought. She could lessen the distance between them quite easily. He was on a high sexual charge already. A gesture from her, a sign, and he'd be unable to hold back. He had the intense passion of all Russian-Hungarians. She could do it. But dared she?

Her nerve gave way. Despite all her reasoning, she couldn't bring herself to walk into his arms. And then her eyes focused on an arbour, drunken with ruby-red roses like those Tanya had carried in her wedding bouquet. A sob rose in her throat. Somewhere on a tropical island, Tanya and István were struggling to enjoy their honeymoon. She was overwhelmed with the desperately urgent feeling that she must ring them and put their minds at rest and she couldn't do that until she'd won László around.

Being kissed, suffering the bitter-sweet pleasure of the tantalising crawl of his hands over her body, was nothing in comparison to the need to stop the terrible hurt inside her. And with his daughter and the baby coming back, he wouldn't dare to go too far.

She felt a stab of pain in her hand and looked down. Unconsciously she had clutched at a stake that was supporting some tall hollyhocks, and had punctured her skin with a rusty piece of wire that had been looped around it. She rubbed at the smear of blood absent-mindedly, her mind on other things.

Ridiculously, she didn't know how to start. Flirting—making a pass—wasn't something she knew about. Nervously she turned and sought out László. He'd walked deeper into the garden and was standing beside a foxglove tree, one hand lifted to enclose a slender branch above his head, the arc of his arm, the line of his body frighteningly appealing to her.

'OK. You win,' she said huskily. 'I'll stay. I'll meet your family and——'

His back remained rigid. 'Agree to marry me.'

The blood pounded in her body and for a moment she couldn't breathe. Even knowing it was a farce, she felt swamped by the enormity of what he wanted her to say. Her eyes filled. This wasn't how she'd imagined it.

'Yes,' she whispered.

'Fine.'

He'd exhaled the vast breath he'd been holding as though his troubles were almost over. Hers had begun, she thought unhappily and driven by that knowledge, her hesitant hand touched his arm and he jerked, whirling around so that she found herself facing his chest. 'László,' she faltered, her throat dry with nerves. Snagging her lower lip in her teeth, she rested her slender fingers on his hard body. The flesh beneath the fine linen shirt was warm from the sun and she could feel the heavy thud of his heart.

'You're bleeding!' He took her hand and turned it over, gently investigating her soft palm. 'How did you do that?' he enquired gruffly.

'On some rusty wire,' she said jerkily.

Lifting her hand, he licked the small wound clean with a few slow sweeps of his tongue. Numb with tension, Suzanne gazed wide-eyed at the thickly springing black hair, an inch or two away and wondered what force was drawing her mouth towards the smooth, tanned brow. The sensation on her hand took over. László had pressed his mouth deep into the soft flesh and was sucking, his face deeply absorbed in the task.

She thought of his mouth on her breast. And gave a little gasp of helpless desire.

'We must find some sage and yarrow,' he said quietly, dabbing her hand dry. Carefully he curled her fingers over and enclosed them in his. 'Though I've probably prevented any infection.' He smiled faintly. 'Nothing like the human mouth, is there?'

Suzanne couldn't focus her mind properly. Somehow her breasts were suddenly touching his chest, the nipples thickening and lengthening in an instant. And as she breathed, fast and shallow, she could feel them rubbing in an unbearably rapid rhythm that sent shock-waves through her taut nerves and made her want to stay there, enjoying the sensation, instead of drawing away as any nice girl would.

'Oh, Suzanne,' he muttered.

Her fingers made their own way up to the beating pulse at his throat. 'I'm confused,' she admitted in a small, defenceless voice that needed no acting to make it that way. And she met the breathtaking darkness of his eyes.

She didn't know how long they stood there, looking at each other. Only that, by the time he gave a muted growl and took her in his arms, she was confused no longer. Her infatuation with him was total. Enemy or not, ruthless manipulator, hell-bent on vengeance or not, she'd fallen head-over-heels for him and there was absolutely nothing she could do about it.

'I don't think I should be doing this,' he said huskily.

'I wish I weren't,' she whispered, aghast at her feeling of euphoria. 'I'd prefer to hate you——'

'I'd prefer it too. But you don't.' His mouth found hers and she sank into him, letting her body blend and fuse with his. 'You smell so sweet,' he breathed, nibbling her ear gently. 'Sweet....' She opened her mouth to his, throwing her arms around his neck in a mindless frenzy, desperate to feel his hard body against hers, the erotic tug of his teeth on her willing lips. 'And oh, how passionate!'

His hand slid to the naked flesh of her back, crushing her to him. Somewhere in her mind she remembered the reason for getting so close to him—other than because she wanted it more than anything. If she had any sense, she'd be putting the brakes on soon, but...not yet. She needed to...

Her mind went blank. Left to its own devices, her body responded eagerly, driven by the seductive plundering of his mouth. Murmuring her appreciation, she cradled his head in her hands and drove his mouth more fiercely into hers, writhing her body luxuriously against his in an instinctive movement.

The effect was electrifying. László shuddered and drew in a sharp breath, then pushed her back and fixed her with his black, well-deep gaze. And she read one thing in them: danger. Before she could find where her voice had disappeared to, he had scooped her up in his arms and was striding purposefully towards one of the barns.

'László!' she croaked, pushing ineffectually against his chest.

'We have to,' he growled, smothering her face with impassioned kisses. 'Unless we do, we'll never be able to get on with our lives. Once, just this once, Suzanne. Then we'll be sane.' Burying his head in her throat, he kissed her with such brutal gentleness that she was shaken into silence. 'I won't hurt you. It will be wonderful,' he murmured against her shimmering skin. 'But,' he grated, 'I must make love to you——'

'But——'

His eyes blazed into hers and she cringed to see that he'd gone beyond all control. 'It's the best way,' he muttered harshly. 'For both of us.'

He kicked open the door and then darkness engulfed them. Suddenly she was being lowered. Soft hay cushioned her body then László covered her. 'Ohhhh,' she whispered, before she knew she'd even opened her mouth.

'I know,' he said softly touching her hair. 'I know. You see,' he murmured, deftly undoing her shirt buttons, 'our bodies have needed each other from the moment we met.'

Three buttons, she thought dizzily. Two more to go. 'Why?' she wailed. 'I don't want this——'

László smiled, and enclosed her mouth in his, persuading her that she did want it, very much. Hands spread over her body, exploring, undressing. Her pulses quickened to his touch while her flesh yielded unconditionally. Only her mind was fighting. Logic told her that this was right, that once they'd sated their bodies they could rid themselves of the gnawing hunger and...

She frowned, trying to remember the point she'd been trying to make to herself. But László's mouth was savaging her bare shoulder, the sweet smell of hay was all around her and she needed him so badly that her hands were frantically pulling open his shirt, freeing it with

unseemly haste and—oh, she groaned quietly to herself,
his body was beautiful.

Her mouth nuzzled his satin skin. Smooth, soft beneath her lips. Nice to taste. Tentatively she flicked her
tongue along the collarbone and felt a thrill of excitement when he quivered.

'Suzanne,' he said hoarsely.

'I've not—not gone this far before,' she mumbled,
intent on tracing the contours of his chest with her lips
and fingers.

'Hell!' he breathed. 'Oh, sweet hell! Come here,' he
growled, and rolled over with her, dragging off her skirt,
his fingers finding the soft, warm skin above her stocking
top. And then the curve of her buttock.

His hand stilled. She felt his body lose its flowing li-
quidity and turn into a frozen statue. Her heavy lids
fluttered open. 'László?'

In a swift movement, he rolled away, gained his feet
and stuffed his shirt back into his trousers. 'I'm crazy,'
he muttered. 'I'm out of my mind.'

Suzanne covered her face with her hands in horror.
She'd invited him to make love to her—and he'd rejected her! He must despise her for being so cheap, so
available! Why had she done that? Madness. No other
reason. With a moan, she buried her head in the hay
and began to sob brokenly.

His hand touched her back but she shrank away. 'No!
Don't touch me!' she raged. 'I—I didn't want you,' she
said stubbornly, denying the obvious. 'I wanted you to—
to see me as a woman——'

'I do,' he frowned. 'That's the problem. I'd prefer to
see you as a means to an end. You're making it very
difficult for me, Suzanne.' His head lifted and for a
moment he remained quite still, listening. 'I can hear a
car,' he said huskily. 'It'll be my daughter. Can you tidy
yourself here?'

She nodded dumbly, refusing to meet his eyes. 'Mmm.'

László gently tipped up her chin. He wasn't cynical
or mocking—or even triumphant. Instead he seemed

quite... tender. She felt her stomach swoop and silently begged him not to look so *lovable*.

'God damn you,' he whispered. And bent to kiss her with such infinite sweetness that she couldn't hold back her moan of despair and wanting, or the artless rise of her hands to the beautiful curve of his strong jaw. 'I must go,' he said shakily. 'And later, we're going to talk. We can't continue like this. I can't keep my hands off you, however hard I try. You're a Jezebel and the trouble is that you don't even know it.' Serious-faced, he gently lifted away her caressing fingers. 'If my attraction for you was only sex,' he muttered, 'I wouldn't mind. That, I could deal with. Unfortunately, I think it's more than that. Dammit,' he said hoarsely. 'I'm feeling a little insane. The wine...'

And he'd gone. Suzanne lay back in the hay and stared up at the wooden beams of the barn, trying to piece her mind together. She felt crazy, too, and that scared her. The two of them were on the edge of something that could tip them over into behaviour they didn't welcome.

Yet... Hearing the car more clearly now, she postponed the thought that had popped into her mind, sat up and busied herself with arranging her clothes. Her hair would be more difficult to tidy. She decided to release it entirely from the snood since so much of it was flowing loose already. Shaking her head violently to rid herself of any betraying straw, she coaxed her hair to lie flat and straight, letting it flow down over her back and shoulders.

Yet... Even though she'd compromised herself by her cheap and easy surrender, it had achieved the result she'd sought. In László's eyes had been a need that went beyond sex—and he'd admitted as much.

Peering into a reflective window-pane, she frantically smoothed her thick eyebrows and checked that her mascara hadn't smudged. Her lipstick was non-existent, but László's kisses had engorged her mouth and given it a natural rose of its own. She'd have to do. Probably his daughter was used to women wandering out of the garden in a state of confusion, she thought wryly.

Before leaving, she stilled her mind. It would be possible to turn László from his course. But to do that, she'd have to give more of herself. And she wasn't sure she dared risk that. An inborn feminine instinct told her that any surrender to László would carry with it an explosion of emotion between them that would turn her ordered life into a turmoil.

And logic mitigated against such a stupid action.

CHAPTER NINE

THE noise, when she came nearer to the house, was quite startling. It made her think wistfully of the days at home when they'd all been talking at once while gathered around the kitchen table. Suddenly she felt a little shy. It wouldn't be easy, meeting László's daughters. Ruefully, she acknowledged that it would make her relationship with him even more complicated.

Taking a deep breath, she strode into the kitchen. For a moment, the babble of languages continued and she tried to sort people out, but everyone stopped talking before she could do so and stared at her curiously and she wondered if he'd told them they were 'engaged'. His next words suggested he hadn't, much to her relief.

'Suzanne,' said László casually. 'I've been telling the girls about your new venture. I don't think they've been listening,' he said with fatherly cynicism. 'They've been far too intent on telling me about *their* activities today.'

'I'm Dinah. This is Lara. Hello!'

Feeling awkward, but reassured by the warmth of Dinah's welcome, Suzanne shook hands with the two young women who stared at her with their mother's laughing mouth and friendly face.

'You never said she was beautiful,' accused Lara.

László's eyes flickered. 'Meet Nikki,' he murmured, expertly detaching a dark-eyed baby from a portable car-seat and placing him in her arms.

Suzanne was too wrapped up in László's heart-stopping expression of tenderness for Nikki to demur, till it was too late. There she was, a baby in her arms beaming up at her expectantly. What did she do? She felt reduced to total inadequacy for once in her life. He burped and a small trickle of milk shot from his mouth

147

on to his *Jungle Book* T-shirt. No one rushed forward to do anything and she looked at it in alarm.

'I don't know how to handle babies——' she began nervously.

'They're like men,' said Dinah in a replica of László's offhand drawl. 'Give them a bit of security, a bit of danger and oodles of body-contact and you'll be OK.'

'Such wisdom in one so young,' mocked László. Leaning forwards, his smooth, golden jaw inches from Suzanne's enormous eyes, he dabbed at the dribble with a piece of towelling and deftly lifted the obliging baby's chin to check the folds of skin beneath.

'For a man with straw in his hair, you're remarkably composed,' retorted Dinah.

Suzanne and László exchanged alarmed glances while the two women fell into fits of laughter. 'We were——' she began in blushing agitation.

'Kissing in the barn and it's no business of yours,' drawled László, quite unconcerned at being found out. 'Nikki's heavy. Sit down, Sue,' he said gently, and his supporting hand guided her to a chair.

Gratefully, she bent her glowing face over the baby. 'I ought to ring and say I'll be delayed for dinner,' she mumbled. And then had a brainwave. 'Or perhaps Dinah could take me back later,' she said more brightly.

'But you promised to stay the night,' he said smoothly. 'We agreed.' She saw the menace in his eyes and cringed. 'If you go, I suppose I could spend the evening making phone calls——'

'No,' she said hastily. 'I'll stay.'

He smiled in triumph. 'That's OK, isn't it, Dinah? We're making an early start in the morning and blinding a few companies with our business acumen,' he explained.

'Knowing you, I expect you'll be blinding them with a takeover bid and handing the shares to the workers,' said Lara, sweeping her arm over the table to clear a space for a plate of walnut cake.

'Go and do your piano practice,' László said in fond rebuke. 'I'll ring the castle for you, Suzanne——'

'No! I——'

'I'll do it,' he said flatly. His eyes warned her not to argue, and, since she was literally left holding the baby and there didn't seem to be a space to put him down, she merely tightened her mouth in annoyance.

'Bossy, isn't he?' Lara said irreverently, when her father had left the room. 'He loves action. Hardly sits still a second.' She cut a huge slab of cake and handed it, without a plate, to Suzanne, who stopped waggling her earrings at the baby and managed to free a hand to take the slice.

Dinah giggled. 'She looks a bit stunned!' she said sympathetically. 'Dad has that effect on people. Don't think you're unusual. He sweeps them into his life and they feel they've been hit by a tornado. Are you sleeping with him tonight? I need to know about beds.'

'No! Certainly not!' Suzanne looked at Dinah in horror. An awful, twisting jealousy was raging through her. Judging by his daughter's reaction, women must often turn up for the night!

'Sorry,' said Dinah hastily. She hesitated and then touched Suzanne on the arm in an apologetic gesture. 'I should have guessed from the way he looked at you that you weren't a casual pick-up,' she said warmly. 'I've never seen him so soft-looking, not since Mum died.'

Suzanne was still frowning over Dinah's assumption that her father only invited women back as sleeping partners. 'Does...does he sleep around, then?' she blurted out, helpless to prevent herself from asking.

'I doubt it. He's awfully uptight. He's never brought any woman here before,' mused Dinah thoughtfully. 'I only asked because I didn't want to spoil his fun. He could do with some.'

'Umm,' munched Lara, nodding her head vigorously. 'Most women are eager to be his conquests. Aren't you?'

'No!' she said hastily, ridiculously cheered by the information about his women.

Dinah and Lara tried to hide their disbelief. 'Don't worry about us. We love him too much to be possessive. He needs someone special to love,' said Dinah firmly.

Her eyes narrowed in warning. 'Don't hurt him. He's been through hell.' Unaware of Suzanne's thoughtful silence, she took her son, hugged him, threw him into the air till he squealed with pleasure and then cuddled him close. 'I'm going to settle him down for the night and have a quick bath,' she announced. 'When I've sorted out a room for you, I'll give you a yell and you can come up and choose a nightie. Unless you never wear one?'

Suzanne went pink. 'I do. But let me help——' But Dinah had gone.

'She's like Dad,' mumbled Lara, nibbling off a layer of walnut topping. 'Takes charge. He can't accept help either. They're so used to fending for themselves.'

'I see. How do you deal with that?' Suzanne frowned.

Lara grinned. 'Give them help whether they like it or not! Mum let me in on that secret when I'd complained about being the youngest in the family and always last in the queue.' Suzanne smiled to herself. László had been quite aware of his younger daughter's problem. 'Of course, I know why Dinah's so capable; she's the eldest and took over when Mum died. Dad's stubborn independence comes from his background. Mum told us about that.'

'Oh? What—what about his background?' asked Suzanne, her wide, almond-shaped eyes fixed nervously on Lara's.

'He had to fend for himself when his family was split up,' answered Lara. 'Ask him about it.' She smiled to herself. 'I suppose that's what makes him such a good father: he knows what it's like not to have one around. Anyway, his in-built caution makes it difficult for people outside the family to get anywhere near the real person. You seem to have twigged that he's got a heart, despite his determination to keep that a state secret.' She giggled. 'I'm much more open, like Mum,' she said affectionately. 'Easy-going, charming, generous, loving...'

Suzanne laughed at Lara's list of assets. 'Your mother looks lovely in the photos I've seen,' she ventured.

'The best,' said Lara gently. 'She and Dad were very much in love.' A sharp pang of jealousy shot through Suzanne's heart and almost instantly she felt ashamed and mean-minded. She was glad László had known happiness. 'Poor Dad. He's got so much love locked up inside. We're not enough for him. He needs someone to share his life with.'

Refraining from disillusioning Lara and saying that László was more concerned with revenge and his sexual frustration, she said, 'You don't mind talking about your mother. You and your sister seem remarkably well-balanced.'

'If we are, it's because of Dad,' explained Lara. 'He told us always to remember her with pleasure and to think of the good times we had together because some families never even had those.'

Emboldened by Lara's relaxed smile, Suzanne nodded. 'I lost my mother when I was a teenager. I know how hard that can be if she's the core of the family.'

'Oh, Dad was the core, always was, always will be,' Lara said surprisingly. 'Tea?' She went to a Russian samovar, returning after a moment with a glass of tea. Popping a generous slice of lemon into the glass, she said tenderly, 'We all worship Dad. Mum did too, of course. Losing *him* would have been worse, I think, because he's always been such a rock to us all.'

'Did he take your mother's death hard?' probed Suzanne.

'Difficult to say. He never showed it—though he stopped laughing. He pulled us together,' she said quietly. 'Got us around the table, made us talk out our misery and anger, told us that whatever happened he'd never put anything or anyone before us. He meant it, too,' she said with a fond smile. 'We ring him up when we need him and sometimes—like when Dinah almost lost Nikki when she was seven months—he jumps in his plane and flies across the world to be with us. That's the kind of man he is: loving, giving, funny and the best——'

'Most thorough beater of slack-mouthed children in the world,' drawled László.

Lara grinned saucily at her father. 'Don't you hate the way he materialises and vanishes?' she groaned. 'He learnt that from the gypsies in Russia.'

'Gypsies?' queried Suzanne in surprise.

'Lara! Piano practice!' growled László.

'OK,' she said amiably. 'Who's doing dinner?'

'Suzanne and me,' he said shortly, wandering to the freezer and opening the lid.

'God! You two, trying to get a meal? With time out for slow, meaningful looks, that could take *hours*!' groaned Lara and ducked out of the room before László's carefully aimed individual fruit pie could hit her.

Amused despite her embarrassment at Lara's remark, Suzanne stood up, ready to help. But first she needed to know about the phone call. 'What did you say to the countess?' she demanded nervously.

'I spoke to Vigadó.' László's eyes were veiled. 'He was furious, I'm delighted to say. He accused me of abducting you.'

'You reassured him?' she asked anxiously.

'No. Of course I didn't. I want him to stew.'

'You told him . . .' She licked her lips.

'Don't do that,' he muttered. 'Yes. I told him.'

Her mouth went dry. 'And?' she prompted, her heart hammering in her chest.

'He's a publisher,' he said shortly. 'He has a remarkable range of curses.' László's lashes fluttered at her moan of dismay. 'He's tearing his hair out. But I think he'll accede to my demands to save you from what he considers to be your infatuation with me.' He gave her a long, slow look. 'He thinks marriage to me would be hell. What do you think?'

Dumb with misery, she couldn't answer. It would be hell and heaven. And almost worth the hell to know the heaven. She swallowed and forced herself to speak. 'He'll call the police!' she grated.

'He has no idea where I might be. And anyway, I advised him not to,' he said, with a sinister smile.

'Because?'

He reached out and touched her pouting lips. 'I said that if he didn't swear on his honour not to, I'd make sure that, by force or by seduction, you'd lose your virginity by the time they'd caught up with me,' he purred.

Incensed, she took a snatch-bite at his finger but he was too quick, darting back with the speed of a snake. Which he was. 'You arrogant devil!' she seethed. 'Why won't you tell me what grudge you've got against Vigadó?'

László was motionless for a moment, lines of strain drawing at his mouth. 'Grudge? Oh, it's more than that. Much more. Do you think I'd waste my time otherwise? He's involved in this deal up to his neck,' he said, a softly lethal growl underlying the words.

'This deal! I'm tired of your games,' she said wearily.

'I wish that were what they were.' He leaned heavily against the wall as though all the stuffing had been knocked out of him. 'I wish to God my father had never set foot in Hungary,' he said bleakly.

'I'm sure the countess would agree with you,' she said in an outburst of temper. He winced and she felt immediately ashamed for some unfathomable reason. He deserved as good as he gave. 'Why don't you leave Hungary?' she said sadly. 'Forget your need for this petty victory over István and Vigadó and just enjoy the love of your family.'

'If only I could!' he growled.

She caught his arm impatiently. 'You can, László! It's perfectly simple. All you have to do is to walk away!'

'Let's get supper,' he said tightly. 'Or we'll have a revolution on our hands.'

'Damn you!' she muttered.

He drew her close. Violently drove his mouth on hers. Forced her around so that she was pressed against the wall, with nowhere to go. Then pushed her away as if he was disgusted with himself, a string of Russian expletives whispered under his breath.

For several seconds he remained motionless, breathing heavily. And then, when he'd come under control, he said coldly, 'For the sake of my kids, I think we should

remain as civilised as possible under the circumstances.
They might come in at any moment. I'd prefer us to be
discussing some uncontroversial topic.'

'Why?' she asked belligerently. 'Why do you bother
to protect them from the fact that I loathe you?'

He gave her an odd look. 'I want us all to enjoy the
meal and not get indigestion. We're stuck with each
other. We don't have to spend all evening fighting.'

'No,' she sighed, admittedly feeling heartily tired of
conflict. A glimpse of his happy family life had made
her feel quite sentimental and in need of a quiet life—
if only for a few hours. 'I'll help you get supper,' she
said in resignation. 'But don't imagine I like you any
better merely because I'm not arguing.'

She pursed her lips, thinking of something uncontroversial to talk about, and saw him lifting a basket of
herbs from the chest freezer. 'Are those for cooking?'
she asked curiously, going to the sink to wash her hands.

'And medicine.' László lifted each variety in turn.
'Borage flowers for salad, these roots for Ferenc's rheu-
matism, sage for a sedative, hyssop for bruises, dill for
fish, lavender for the bath, basil for tomatoes, rosemary
for the linen with the lavender, verbena for everything
you can think of——'

Suzanne paused on the way to the kitchen towel.
'Gypsies,' she said suddenly. 'You learnt all that from
the gypsies! When, László? How?'

'The Romani—the gypsies, as you call them—taught
me how to survive,' he said wryly, hauling a huge package
from the freezer and scanning the label. 'Game pie. OK?'
Without waiting for an answer, he pointed to a sack of
potatoes. 'Get peeling.'

'When and how?' she asked, standing her ground.

He shot her an irritable glance. 'When my father died.
I was an impressionable teenager.' He frowned, his lashes
thickly clustering on his cheekbones so that she couldn't
see the expression in his eyes. Judging by the absent-
minded way he was ripping off the foil from the pie, he
was lost in the past.

'I'm peeling,' she said encouragingly.

'Yes. OK. I suppose it's as good a subject as any to be discussing.' With the manner of a man used to coping with a hungry family, he put the pie in a catering-size microwave to defrost, gathered great handfuls of carrots from a rack and began to clean them up in the double sink beside Suzanne. 'By dying, my father had failed in a task he'd been set. Our family was disgraced overnight. I don't know what happened to my grandparents.' He grimly snapped a carrot in half and stared at it in surprise.

'You mean they vanished?' she cried in horror.

'They went to a camp,' he said shortly. 'I never saw them again.'

'And they'd brought you up,' she said gently. 'Oh, László! You loved them!'

'Yup.'

There was a long silence which she knew better than to interrupt. But she thought of his deep love for his children and knew he must have felt great affection for his grandparents who'd given him such a happy childhood. In the back of her mind was the knowledge that he was a considerate and loving man beneath the cold, hard exterior. It gave her comfort. He couldn't fail to see that it was cruel to split a family in two. She must remind him at the first opportunity.

'How did you feel about that?' she ventured gently.

'Distraught.'

All she could see was his hands, chopping the carrots as if he wanted to decapitate those who'd been in power at the time. He'd been dumped, she thought. Thrown to the wolves.

'So... what did you do?' she asked after a while.

'Disappear,' he replied wryly. 'I joined a *kumpania*— a group—of Romani. They taught me how to live off the land, to trust no one, to love music and to hide my feelings. I learnt to love the outdoors, to hate being cooped up and how to eviscerate rabbits in seconds,' he added with a crooked grin.

She smiled back at him, wanting to ease his bad memories. His revelations had explained a lot about him. 'Sounds fun.'

'A good training ground,' he admitted, still slicing the carrots with admirable accuracy—but a little less vehemence. 'The Romani survive because they know how to read people. They've learnt to understand the human mind, how it ticks—and its fickle nature. When I decided to try my luck in America, they provided me with false papers in the name of Lázár. And that gift of understanding human frailties and behaviour proved to be highly valuable.' The knife poised in mid-air. 'My skill is in having a finger on the pulse of the money markets, a sixth sense. I know when people will run scared and when they'll try to retreat and safeguard their backs. The Romani gave me a future and for that I'm eternally grateful. You ought to be wearing an apron,' he said laconically.

She let him slip one over her head. Lifting her arms, she waited while he tied the strings. But he sensed the trembling of her body and took a step forward, his hands sliding around her waist. 'Don't,' she said shakily, wanting to lean back against him. She could hear Lara playing, a passionately emotional piece that caught her heart. 'I don't want... Not with your children here,' she pleaded.

His mouth brushed her neck. 'They wouldn't mind. They'd object if we delayed their dinner, though!' With evident reluctance, he released her and they continued to prepare the meal in silence, broken only by the beautiful music wafting through the open door.

'Lara plays like a professional,' she observed quietly.

'She's making music her career,' László replied, his voice soft with pride.

'And that,' she said, lifting her head, 'is how you know people at Lisa's music school!'

'I'm on the board of governors.'

'You're full of surprises,' she said thoughtfully.

'Only to those who believe second-hand gossip,' he muttered bitterly.

Her heart lifted. Maybe István and Vigadó were wrong about him. She struggled with the fact that she wanted them to be wrong, for it all to end happily, like a modern-day fairy-tale.

'You have a hard time with the Press?' she asked shrewdly.

He shrugged. 'A few snipers are lying out there, waiting,' he said cynically. 'I've come a long way and made a lot of enemies. They explain their own failure—and what appears to be my uncanny knack of judgement—by hinting that I succeed through corruption and bribery.' He snorted angrily. 'It doesn't occur to them that I'm successful because I spend hours studying the markets, or trying to understand the global picture. You'll need to do a lot more potatoes than that,' he muttered, when she began to search for a saucepan large enough.

'How many people are we feeding?' she asked, askance.

'Dinah's husband will be here, Ferenc and his wife. Where was I? Global picture. Yes. I make some spectacular killings on the markets. It's got to the state that if I sell dollars or sterling or diamonds then everyone else does, too.'

'You're very powerful, aren't you?' she mused.

He shrugged. 'Power attracts envy. That's why I keep a low profile. You become vulnerable to threats. Making a profit seems to have become a dirty word.'

'It depends what you do with your money,' she said.

'I don't rush around telling everyone about my good deeds and donations to charity so they assume I don't make any.'

'But you must do, don't you?' she asked anxiously, hoping. 'You make a lot of money—and yet you say you have nothing——'

'I have my children. You can see what they mean to me, can't you?' he said huskily, eyeing the clutter on the dresser, where a big family photograph took pride of place. 'It's like the Tower of Babel here, sometimes.'

Later, Suzanne felt like an inhabitant of the Tower of Babel. Supper was more enjoyable than she could ever have imagined. Dinah's husband Jo turned out to be an American with a wicked sense of humour who worked for László and she saw immediately why Dinah had fallen for him. The young woman had a maturity beyond her years. It touched her how László deferred to her at times, how his eyes met those of his daughters and were filled with love.

Ferenc's wife had brought an enormous fruit pudding to add to the home-made summer jellies and it was obvious that this was a common arrangement. The clutter, the happy laughter and the cosiness of the big kitchen made Suzanne's defences melt away. It was a moment to cherish. Something for her memory banks.

Her soft, dark hazel eyes turned solemnly to László. He'd just asked Lara her opinion on the latest United Nations action. Everyone else was chipping in with their thoughts on it, but he was listening intently to what his youngest daughter had to say as if it was the most important opinion of all.

She smiled to herself. It was, of course. Making the youngest in the family feel valued was the act of a loving, caring father. Her heart warmed to him. His eyes feasted with deep affection on Lara—on all his family. Suddenly she felt short of breath, the thudding of her heart loud in her ears, and she felt it lurch with some intense, overwhelming feeling that made her feel as if she would burst.

'Suzanne?' came László's voice from the hazy distance. 'More pudding?'

It's this Hungarian wine, she thought dazedly. It's making me sentimental. I look around and remember my own family meals and... She blinked, her eyes resting on László's softened, smiling face. 'No,' she said huskily. The wine... it's making me think I'm falling in love, she thought. He's only a good-looking man. This is only a nice family. I'm drunk.

A slight frown drew his dark brows together over the bridge of his nose. His lashes fluttered then were still, his beautiful, eloquent eyes a little troubled as they probed into her soul. 'You've only drunk half a glass of wine,' he said quietly. 'Isn't it to your taste? Would you like something else instead?'

A kiss, she thought wildly. And had she drunk so little? Her stomach hollowed. Then she wasn't drunk—so what was the matter with her? A fever. He reached across the table and touched her hand. His was hotter than hers. No fever. Frantically she tried to deny the truth.

But it burst into her consciousness like exploding fireworks. Oh, God! she thought! She *was* falling in love with him!

The rest of the evening was difficult. Every time she looked across the comfortable sitting-room towards László, it was to see some evidence of his charm, warmth, affection, generosity, humour... Suzanne scowled. She was making him out to be only marginally less perfect than a saint, whereas he was ruthlessly exploiting her and therefore more akin to a cold-blooded snake.

Much later, in the night, she gave up trying to sleep and decided to sneak downstairs and make a hot drink. Anything to stop her mooning over László, she thought resentfully, slipping into Jo's voluminous Paisley dressing-gown. And heard a wail as she tiptoed across the landing.

It came from behind a door festooned with rabbits and elephants and a carefully painted name-plate with Nikki's name on it so she quietly turned the handle to see if the little boy was all right.

László was there, rocking the wakeful child, softly singing to him in a throaty, heartbreakingly tender voice and as she watched him, his lashes heavy on his prominent cheekbones, she knew without a doubt that she loved this man, whatever, whoever he was, whatever his motives or his deeds and that she loved him with a passion that swelled her heart and made her want to run to him and hold him tight, never to let him go.

'Come and see,' whispered László.

She froze. He'd given no sign that he'd known she was there. The Romani had a lot to answer for! she thought resentfully. And because the man she loved had asked, she went. 'Oh, he's so sweet!' she breathed. 'Is there anything as beautiful as a sleeping child?'

Gently László placed the baby back in his cot and wound up the mobile of woolly lambs and fluffy ducks above it. A lullaby began to play, making her smile.

'Yes,' he said softly. 'There is something as beautiful. You, right now.'

'László!' she mumbled. But he'd taken her hand. He knew it was trembling, that she was weak and full of longing.

He took her silently in his arms and she sighed as her head came to rest on his heart because it sounded as though he felt as emotionally moved as she was. 'We can't do this,' he said thickly, drawing away. 'I can't allow you near me——'

'No,' she whispered, her eyes huge with yearning.

'I mustn't waver in my determination to use you as a bargaining point,' he rasped.

'I've said I'll go along with what you want to do,' she said stiffly. A jerky sob came from deep inside her. 'I've let you pretend that we're—we're getting married!' she mumbled miserably.

László bent to the cot and kissed the child's softly flushed cheek. 'Oh, God!' he groaned softly. 'I'd kill for him!'

'What is it, László?' she whispered in alarm, alerted to the anguish in his voice. 'What's hurting you?'

He couldn't answer for a moment. Then he managed to control his emotions though when he spoke his voice was hoarse with strain. 'My children are being threatened.'

'Oh, no!' she gasped in horror. 'I couldn't bear it if anything happened to any one of them!'

He turned slowly to her. 'I'd do anything. Anything, to keep them safe,' he said and she had the strange feeling that he was trying to tell her something.

'Oh, László!' she whispered, with a quick look at the sleeping child. How sweet Nikki was! she thought, with a rush of loving feeling. 'That anyone would want to harm him...' Her stricken eyes lifted and she scanned László's haggard face. 'Some crank, I suppose,' she said shakily. 'People are always wanting to abduct the children of the wealthy. How terrible! I understand why you want to keep a low profile, why you hide them away here! No one knows they're here, do they?'

'No.' He grabbed her arms roughly, his face dark with menace. 'And you won't tell anyone, will you? Not even your family. Swear to it, Suzanne!'

'Of course!' she cried. 'I'd never reveal it. I wouldn't jeopardise the safety of your children, László,' she said fervently. 'But...what else are you doing about the threats? Have you told the police?'

He stared at her long and hard, the lines of his mouth cruel. But his eyes... She caught her breath. There was a lacerating pain in them. 'I'm handling it,' he said hoarsely.

'Oh, László!' she said in a choking voice. The tears filled her eyes and two huge drops slid on to her cheeks. 'It must be so terrible for you!'

'Don't look at me like that,' he growled savagely. He thrust her away and she half-staggered with the suddenness of his movement. 'I think you'd better go to bed,' he grated.

'Not yet,' she said quietly, remembering what Lara had said. László found it hard to accept help. But she could at least talk to him till he'd relaxed a little. 'Come and walk in the garden or something,' she said persuasively. 'You need——'

'I need sex,' he said harshly. 'A fierce, wild, passionate night with an athletic, inventive woman.' His angry eyes flipped up to sear hers with their lethal flames. 'Are you willing?'

She shrank back in panic. 'No!' she whispered. 'You know I'm not! László, you don't know what you're saying—in front of your grandchild——'

'I know exactly what I'm saying,' he replied in measured terms. The bitter lines of his mouth destroyed the pureness of his dark profile against the pale wall and she saw how merciless he could be when he wanted. And shivered. The coal-black eyes were veiled now, holding her paralysed where she stood. 'That's the only kind of relief I want now. Something intensely physical. I don't want sympathetic chats or logic or your gentle nurturing,' he snarled softly. His teeth bared hungrily. 'Give me a night of sex or, for the love of God, keep away.'

Her mouth trembled. He was in pain and taking it out on her. She wanted desperately to comfort him but couldn't offer him what he needed—and that hurt more than anything. Tears streamed down her cheeks as she stood there, unmoving. And eventually he drew in a huge, shuddering breath and strode angrily outside, leaving her feeling as if she'd been standing in the centre of a tornado.

There came the sound of hoofbeats; a man, riding hard and fast. And she knew that he'd found a physical release for his anguish and slowly returned to her own room to wait for the dawn.

Tired, edgy, she emerged for breakfast the next morning in an old robe of Dinah's and if he noticed the dark circles beneath her eyes then he never commented in the hurly burly of getting Lara off to school and with Nikki and Dinah leaving to visit friends.

Then she and László were alone. The silence made her tense and she jumped when he finally spoke.

'I arranged for your suit to be pressed,' he said curtly. 'Ferenc's wife has washed and ironed your shirt.' He jerked his head in the direction of the hangers on the back of the door. 'You'll look efficient enough this morning.'

Suzanne frowned. 'You mean we're actually going out, to see these business contacts?' she asked in surprise.

'I made a bargain with you.' He poured himself a coffee. He'd had nothing else, not even when teased by his daughters for foregoing his usual vast, cooked breakfast and Suzanne had squirmed uncomfortably, aware that they were blaming her for his taciturn behaviour.

'I don't know that I can,' she said huskily.

Time in his company. Close to him . . .

'Refuse, and I'll force you,' he said with soft menace.

Her huge, apprehensive eyes searched his, baffled by his insistence. 'You're hurting me,' she whispered.

His mouth twisted and he walked out, leaving the coffee untouched. With robotic movements, she took down the suit and blouse and dressed. He was waiting for her, took her arm firmly and grimly marched her outside. Mute and weary, she resigned herself weakly to the torment.

In the town of Györ, on an eighteenth-century balcony enclosed by a wrought-iron trellis, they discussed quotas with earnest men in bristling moustaches who'd once worked for the massive state textile organisation. In clipped, detached tones, László had reminded her that they must insist on quality checks and uniformity of production for the linen she needed. It took longer than they'd expected before he'd coaxed and negotiated his way to a deal, but his patience had won in the end and she'd been surprised at his gentle, but wickedly subtle methods of bargaining.

Surprised, too by the fond way his eyes had rested on her.

In Sopron, near the Austrian border, they'd walked through the narrow cobbled streets of the medieval town to an office overlooking a courtyard. Here, László had taught her more about communicating ideas, enthusing people and persuasive negotiation than she could have learnt in a lifetime.

And he had patted her hand and touched her more often than was necessary.

Finally, in a small factory in beech woods, she stood amid the clatter of looms, watching the weavers, the shuttles flying in and out, and thought, so many separate threads, weaving together by a complex process, yet making a whole.

Ahead of her was László, his jacket hooked on one finger in the heat, his handsome head bent so that a black-clad widow could yell in his ear. He grinned his dazzling grin, and engaged in some banter that made the woman crack up with laughter.

Soberly Suzanne fingered the samples of material in her hands. Rough, smooth, twisted, straight, exotic, natural: László could be all things to all people. And to her, he was the man she might have spent a lifetime waiting for—but was here, now. The trouble was, he didn't want her, other than for sex, or his distorted exploitation.

'Made your selection?'

She jumped. 'Yes,' she said briskly.

To her amazement, in front of everyone, he tenderly stroked her face, the gesture of a lover. 'We'll go,' he said huskily.

Suzanne was bewildered by his behaviour. In something of a daze, she allowed herself to be led out, conscious of the gazes of everyone there upon them. 'What——?'

His arm came around her. 'Well done,' he said warmly, giving her a hug. 'You did some good work in there. I thought you listened well and watched what was happening in the room, like a true professional. You were in control. I'm proud of you, Suzanne.'

'Oh! Thanks,' she said uncertainly. He'd pulled her hard against his thigh and as they walked to the car she felt their intimacy must be the cause of the murmur behind them. 'László!' she muttered, trying to pull away.

'Don't,' he warned, sliding his hand more firmly around her waist. 'I want them to think we're friendly. My support for you will ensure that they stick to those shrinkage and sleeve tolerances you stood out for.'

'You mean if they think we're—we're——'

'Lovers,' he supplied huskily.

'I don't understand,' she mumbled.

'You don't need to,' he said silkily, turning her around. A light kiss descended on her lips and his eyes blazed when she made to break free. 'Stay, or you lose everything you've gained,' he said under his breath. Then flashed a smile at her, kissed her again and opened the car door.

Dazed, she slid into the soft leather seat. 'You're up to something,' she said sourly, annoyed that he'd made her tremble.

'Smile. Wave cheerfully, put your arm along the top of my seat,' he said, his expression that of a loving partner. '*Do it*!'

She did. He bestowed on her the kind of look she would have given her eye teeth for, had it been deeply meant, and drove off. Almost immediately they'd turned a bend in the road, he reverted to how he'd been at the beginning of the journey: cold, remote, silent.

'If I can only achieve my ends because people think I'm your mistress,' she said coldly, 'then I want nothing of this.'

The car screeched to a halt as László jammed on his brakes violently, jerking her forwards hard before the seatbelt bit into her body. 'You'll do it my way,' he said savagely. 'They will believe there's something between us and they will do anything you want, better than they'll do it for anyone else.'

'Why?' she demanded hotly.

'Because they admire me, they respect me and they like me,' he said grimly.

Yes, she thought. They did. He'd charmed them all, wrapped them around his little finger. 'I don't like it. It's deceitful,' she muttered rebelliously. 'I won't——'

She gasped. He'd caught her shoulders and shaken her. 'What does it matter to you? It's nothing; a smile, a look that lingers longer than normal, a hand around your waist!' he snarled. 'Dammit, Suzanne, do you have to keep throwing your principles at me?'

'I can't compromise on the way I work,' she said grimly.

He was silent, staring at her as though she'd completely thrown him. 'Then I have to admit,' he said huskily, unlatching his seatbelt with alarming intent, 'that it's nothing to do with business.' Her throat went dry as his hand caressed her hair, sliding over the smooth strands with a look of longing on his face that made her heart turn over. 'It's because I've been unable to keep my hands off you,' he whispered. 'And I'm not going to deny myself any longer.'

She opened her mouth to protest and found it where it should be: beneath his. For a moment she made a token protest and then she gave up, slipping her arms around his neck and sinking into the kiss with an abandon that unnerved her.

With a groan, he kicked out with his foot and she found herself flying backwards as the seat took up a reclining position. His eyes glittered into hers as he fumbled by her hip for her seatbelt, then he smiled wickedly. 'On second thoughts,' he murmured, and deliberately left her trapped beneath him.

'We—have work,' she husked, watching the slow, sensual curve of his lips. Her own mouth reached out, touched his, and she let the tip of her tongue explore the chiselled arch, the high bow, the sweep to each side and the firm, fullness below.

'Work,' he agreed hoarsely. But his hands slowly toured her body and she arched and stretched in pleasure as he learnt each dip and swell with agonising slowness.

'Next—appointment,' she croaked.

The blare of a lorry klaxon made them both jump. László bit his lip. 'I want you,' he said, in a tone of sadness. 'I wish I didn't.'

'Do you feel you're betraying what you felt for your wife?' she asked tentatively.

'No.' He gritted his teeth. 'We've got to go, Suzanne,' he said harshly.

Miserably she waited for him to return the seat to the upright position. She felt like a prisoner. Of her emotions, of him... He'd woven a spell around her and she was part of the threads of his life now. Without taking a pair of shears and making a deliberate cut, she'd never escape her feelings for him. And she couldn't do that, because he'd carry out his threat to disinherit István.

'I hate you,' she mumbled unhappily.

'I hate you too,' he growled.

CHAPTER TEN

FOR the rest of the long day, while she pondered over buttons and threads and out-workers, tolerances and quotas, selecting, forcing her mind to stay fixed on the task in hand, his hands and eyes kept returning to her as if drawn by some invisible magnet.

People talked. She could see that. Word would get around. But she couldn't help it; she wanted his touch, the caress of his eyes, more than anything.

'We're going back.'

Suzanne kept her gaze ahead on the horses, galloping on the horizon against a huge, setting sun. She was tired. He'd pushed her beyond her reserves. 'To the castle?' she asked hopefully.

'No. You'll stay at Dinah's for the next few days while we clinch all these deals and tie up all the loose ends,' he replied.

Risking a quick glance, she saw that his profile was hard and uncompromising. 'How far is it before we're there?' she asked wearily. 'We've travelled miles and miles——'

'A long way. And I'm tired too. I'm finding this hard to handle, Suzanne.'

'You're the one who keeps touching me!' she said resentfully.

'You're the one who's walking around looking like an angel and making me wish you were a whore,' he said bitterly.

She clamped her mouth shut at that and watched the road darken as the hours slipped by. László seemed on edge, the muscles in his strong thighs and arms taut and hard. They slowed only to pass through dimly lit villages, the only brightness the white-painted Orthodox churches that loomed up in the dark night.

Several times he swerved on the open road to avoid a cyclist or a homeward farmer and she realised how dangerous the roads were because no one seemed to bother about lights.

László thrust a cassette into the radio and swore. 'It's jammed!' Angrily, he fumbled with it for a moment, narrowly missed a wandering cow and gave up. 'Sing to me.'

'What?' she muttered in surprise.

'Sing. Talk. Anything, or I'll disappear off the road. I'm tired. The road is full of hazards. I'll kill someone if I can't keep sharp.'

So she sang. Anything was better than talking. At first, she felt embarrassed and her voice was feeble, but after a short time he joined in with his wonderful, smoky voice.

Yet he was still very anxious, sitting forwards, peering into the darkness ahead, his speed low. 'We'll take hours to get back,' he complained.

Suddenly, Suzanne screamed. She'd seen the shape of a cart a yard or so ahead. 'Look out! László!' She dived to protect him; he reached out to protect her and they missed the cart by inches, coming to a shuddering stop a short way down the road.

In the silence, they held one another tightly. The cart trundled past, the sound of horse hooves clopping on the tarmac, the wooden wheels squeaking and creaking loudly.

He held her close as if he couldn't bear to let her go and in her foolishness she pretended that he cared. 'I can't go on,' he whispered in her ear.

'No. I can see that. Is there somewhere near we can stay?' she asked shakily.

He began to laugh ruefully. 'Oh, Suzanne!' he sighed. 'That's not what I meant! You're making this very hard for me.' Tenderly he kissed her. 'We'll ask for hospitality at the next village.'

After that, they kept their trips to a minimum. But he still found it impossible to keep from touching her in public. While in private he was aloof and almost rude. It seemed to her that he was two different men and she began to wonder which was the real László. She swung like a pendulum; she loves him, she loves him not. She wanted to leave, she felt compelled to stay.

He had made her swear not to telephone any of her family and because of the possible danger to his children she'd agreed; but she'd written to Tanya and Mariann, telling them about her progress and of László's remarkable business skills.

And, because she badly needed to share her feelings and soften the blow of her presumably inexplicable engagement to him, she told Mariann about the way he was with his children, the funny things they did, the wonderful father he was and it seemed to her that her sentences all began with one word. László.

Her days, her evenings, her nights were a torment. In the work she was doing, she was realising all her ambitions, and yet they were suddenly empty because they would be enjoyed without the love of the man she craved like a drug.

One evening, towards the end of a poignantly hilarious supper, she cracked up. Bursting into tears and silencing them all with the suddenness of it, she cried steadily into her pudding, unable to stop the gush of emotion.

'Out!' said László tersely to everyone.

She sensed their exchange of knowing glances and heard the door close. Sobbing hysterically, she expected him to make some move of conciliation. Sympathy, at least. He just let her cry, sitting as motionless as a stone statue. And then she knew he cared about as much for her as for the untouched pudding on his plate. So she stopped crying, full of anger instead.

'Now we'll go outside,' he said gruffly.

'Like hell we will!' she sniffed.

'I can pick you up and carry you out, I can march you off with one arm wrenched behind your back, or you can go with some dignity,' he said coldly. 'Your choice.'

Her swollen eyes shot venom at him. 'Thanks,' she said sarcastically. 'God, you're a bully!' But she rose and stumbled out behind him into the blackness of the night.

'Mind the hedgehog,' he said curtly over his shoulder.

'*Hedgehog*!' she exploded bitterly, skirting the happily scurrying animal. He cared more for a prickly hedgehog! she thought irrationally.

Suzanne stalked after László into the silent summer warmth, brutally reminded of the time they'd first met in the moonlight. Ill met, she thought unhappily. He stopped by a garden seat where the air hung heavily with the scent of night stock and motioned for her to sit beside him.

She chose to stand.

'I don't think either of us can go on, can we?' he said in a distant tone.

Her heart began to thud. 'You want to withdraw financial support? Or are you referring to our travesty of an engagement?' she asked, her throat dry with alarm.

Her fear wasn't for the lack of backing, though; what she dreaded was parting from him. Torment or not, being with him was better than nothing. She could watch the slow smile, the intent eyes, the pure profile, and soak him up like dye in a cloth, indelibly imprinted with his mark.

'No,' he said shortly. 'I want to explain some of my actions and tell you——' He drew in a long, shaky breath and stared at the ground, his expression brooding. 'To explain about the threats concerning my children.'

'Oh, László!' she cried, immediately concerned. 'Have there been more?'

'When I told you about it,' he said quietly, 'I didn't mean that someone had sent a kidnap note.'

Her eyes narrowed. 'But—you said——'

'No,' he interrupted curtly. 'You said. And I let it ride because I wasn't prepared to tell you the real reason. Now I have to. You're not going to like this——'

'I haven't liked anything you've done,' she said angrily, skimming over the pleasure she'd known merely by being at his side.

He scowled at his feet. 'Vigadó is threatening them.' He looked up to see her reaction.

Her grudging respect for him crumbled to dust. 'Oh, sure,' she said scornfully. 'He's always putting on monster masks and forcing kids to give up their sweeties!

How dare you?' she raged, bristling with fury. 'Vigadó
is one of the most loving——'

He reached out, his eyes chilling, and jerked her
roughly towards him. His grip tightened on her wrist till
she stopped protesting and was reduced to a pained
groan. Slowly she was forced to her knees, his ruthless
gaze holding hers all the while. And she thought miserably, How could I love this man?

'Now listen,' he said softly. 'Don't interrupt. It's very,
very important. I've spent nearly a year working towards
this point and I'm damned if you're going to ruin everything. Understand?' She nodded, wincing and he eased
the pressure around her wrists a little. 'Vigadó is in the
throes of publishing a book,' he said grimly. 'It's a
demolition job on me.'

'In the non-fiction section, then,' she grated.

And was scalded by his lethal eyes. 'This is not a joke!'
he said savagely. 'My ex-partner wrote the book in revenge. I reported the man to the authorities two years
ago for fraud, bribery and corruption. He's serving a
ten-year sentence in a Hong Kong jail.'

'And you're scared your children will discover they've
got a criminal for a father,' she said, her face stiff with
horror. 'László! How could you!' she cried brokenly.

He winced as though she'd driven a knife into his body.
'My ethics are beyond reproach! You think I'd jeopardise their happiness by going beyond the law?' he asked
in a hoarse, strained whisper.

'I don't know what to think!' she moaned, tipping her
head back in despair. 'I can't think any more!'

'I'll give you a moment,' he muttered rawly.

Almost immediately she shook her head. 'No,' she
breathed. 'You wouldn't. I know that. So...' Her voice
tailed away. He was so tense that he was shaking. Her
eyes scanned him in wonder. 'What is it?' she asked
softly, her heart aching. 'Tell me. Share it!'

For a brief second, his hands cupped her uplifted face
and then dropped away, his whole demeanour one of
dejection and despondency. 'Vigadó rightly thinks the
book is dynamite and must be in the public domain,' he
said huskily. 'That means it's a duty to publish it. My
partner has owned up to his association with crooks and

is implicating me as well—because I shopped him, the moment I found out he was crooked.' László's face darkened and his voice became a low, furious and utterly frustrated growl that welled up from deep inside him. 'I was sent a copy of the proofs by the lawyers from the publishing house for my comments. I said I'd sue.'

'Then it won't get published, will it? They won't risk it,' she said slowly.

'I can prove nothing. Nothing!' snarled László. He stood up as though he couldn't contain himself any longer and began to pace up and down. 'He has dates, meetings, contacts, deals—all of which can be substantiated. Only he was the one involved, not me. And he's picked the occasions when I have no alibi, no other proof of my movements; when I've been alone in the forest, riding somewhere on my own, travelling to rendezvous with people in the Eastern Bloc——' He frowned and clamped his lips together. 'He can also show evidence,' he went on, 'of insider dealing on the Stock Exchanges and there's no way I can prove him wrong. His word against mine. And the Press has already sown the seeds of doubt about my honesty and integrity. They'll have a field day.'

'Have you told Vigadó the truth?' she asked.

He gave a short laugh. 'He didn't believe me. Do you know how hard it was for me to go to him and beg, and to have my request for discretion flung back in my face?' he asked bitterly. 'No. If my partner was crooked, I was—by implication. The Hungarians have a saying; the fish rots from the head. Besides, my name was already mud because Vigadó knew I'd caused a hell of a lot of trouble for István.'

'You said you kept your private life low-profile,' she said, feeling his pain acutely. He hated to ask for help but he'd been forced to. 'László, if he knew what you felt about your children, maybe——'

'No!' he roared, shattering her fragile nerves and making her jump. 'I'm not stupid enough to make myself even more vulnerable than I am!'

'But...' She gulped, her face pale with horror. 'You'd be sent to gaol!' The thought of his children without a

father any more, and of the restless, roving, vital László
confined to a prison cell, was too terrible to contemplate.

'Or I'd have to go on the run,' he grated. 'I've had
enough of that to last me a lifetime.'

'An injunction!' she suggested.

'I've tried that,' he said impatiently, 'and failed.' He
stopped pacing for a moment. 'That's why I decided to
use you as my weapon.'

She closed her eyes for a brief, despairing moment.
'I'm beginning to understand,' she said shakily. 'Your
family harmony was being threatened and you'd do anything to safeguard them from harm, from gossip and
Press conjecture.'

'I had a way to make you do what I wanted,' he
muttered.

'Threatening to reveal your identity to István,' she said
bitterly.

He nodded. 'And I'd discovered how close you were
to Mariann. *That* close,' he said, twisting his two fingers
together to show her inseparable bond with her sister.
'Any threat to your long-term happiness, like an association with a renegade like me, would put the fear of
God into your sister. And therefore her fiancé.'

It didn't seem much of a threat. 'You took a gamble,'
she said with a puzzled frown. The odds seemed low for
his success.

'Less of a gamble than you imagine,' he murmured.

There was more, she knew. Something he was still
holding back. 'This was the deal you told me about,'
she said shakily. She sat back and mulled over the rami-
fications and her face went chalk white. From the very
beginning, he'd planned and executed a cold-blooded
scheme to save himself—and to be fair, his children as
well—from the consequences of publication. 'You didn't
want to help me at all,' she said in a small voice.

'I was impressed by you,' he said curtly. 'I admired
your business acumen. But my prime motivation was to
stop publication. I've always been in two minds about
wresting the Huszár estates from István and the countess
for reasons I've already told you. But I was suddenly
given a choice to make and I found myself perfectly prepared to set the land and title aside in exchange for the

suppression of this libellous book. Land has no heart, no emotions to be destroyed. My children have.'

Sympathy poured from her heart, filling her throat and knotting in a small, hard lump that made it difficult to talk. He put his family above everything and she respected him for that.

'You could have threatened Vigadó with that information,' she said, 'instead of involving me. You could have told him you meant to destroy the whole estate if——'

'No,' he said gently. 'I wouldn't have destroyed it.'

'Oh.' That was some relief. Even he couldn't bring himself to be that petty. She felt glad. 'But I still don't understand why you involved me!' she said resentfully.

'I judged that Vigadó would have told me to go ahead, to take the estate. He is probably fond of Tanya and István—but not as deeply tied up with them as you. He hasn't a woman's perception of the intensity of feeling that István and the countess have for that land. He's a man who is too highly principled to be blackmailed. I needed to reach him where he's vulnerable—and the only soft spot where I could wound him deeply is the love of his life; Mariann.' His eyes gleamed. 'Now, since I like to stay above the law,' he said with careful emphasis, 'I wasn't prepared to abduct her, or harm her, or to attempt seduction. So I looked to you, *her* greatest weakness—after her fiancé.'

'Now I understand why you succeed in business,' she breathed. 'Your mind is devious. When you can't find one way around an obstacle, you come at it from a different angle.' She studied his hard, emotionless face in despair. She had to think like him. There must be a way to approach this problem. 'Why don't you wait till after publication and then fight in the courts?' she asked, suddenly hopeful.

'Because my family will have been put through too much speculation and worry and because mud sticks,' he said harshly. 'My business is all about confidence. If I lose that, I lose all control.' He turned glittering eyes on her. 'You have to help me.'

'How?' she muttered.

'By continuing as we are. Keeping to the pretence that
we're in love and planning marriage. It's been hard for
you over the last few days. Me too. But if you know
what I'm up to, maybe it won't be so difficult for us to
handle. That was my reasoning, anyway,' he said his
mouth twisting wryly. 'And I need a stronger
lever——'

'I knew there was something else!' she exclaimed,
twisting her hands nervously.

'Good. You're learning. I want you to let Vigadó and
István think you've already become my mistress.'

She froze as something awful dawned on her. 'Is that
what you've been doing these past few days?' she asked
hoarsely. 'You said—you said it was because you couldn't
keep your hands off me, but——! Oh, God!' she
groaned, shaking her head in an attempt to deny what
he'd done to her. She remembered what he'd said some
time ago; that their relationship had to be publicised,
talked about... 'You brute!' she seethed. 'Snake! Liar,
cold-blooded——'

'I'll do anything to get what I want, as I said,' he told
her coldly. The inhumanity in his expression made her
want to weep. 'My first intention was to get you into my
bed and make the menfolk in your family scared witless
about what was happening to you. Men are notoriously
protective of young virgins in their family,' he said, his
mouth curling sensually. 'And you were *perfect*. You
yourself complained about being seen as the baby of the
family. No doubt István and Vigadó see you that way
too. The thought of a man like me making love to you,
a man of my age introducing you to all the permutations
of sex—well, that would have driven them into a fury.'

'But you didn't get me into bed,' she snapped. And
crushed the thought that she'd been close to surrender
several times.

'You and your high moral standards!' he mocked. 'It
didn't signify. I altered my plans.'

'To what?' she demanded, leaping up to confront him.

A brutal look of challenge. 'To an assault on your
female sentimentality instead,' he growled. 'I in-
troduced you to my family so you would side more
readily with me.'

At the hard, measured tones, her blood went cold. All that loving father stuff, the happy meals they'd eaten together, the affection he'd lavished on his children in front of her, had been a deliberate manipulation of her emotions.

'You used your children? Dear heaven, you were totally conscious of everything you were doing, of all my reactions!' she said hysterically. 'And I'd thought that any reference I might make to family life would soften *you* up and make you care what happened to me and Tanya! I must have been crazy to believe that!'

She turned her back on him, unable to bear the sight of his lying face any more. The caresses they'd shared, the kisses—everything had been part of his Soften Suzanne Up technique. Shame and mortification washed through her like a tidal flood.

She'd fallen in love with a sham.

'I wish I'd never met you!' she cried miserably.

'*God!*'

She whirled around. The word had exploded from inside him and the sheer agony in his eyes cut through her like a knife. Whatever he was doing to her, however much he was hurting her, she wanted to ease his anguish even while she wanted to score her nails down his face and ease her *own* pain. He was tearing her in two.

'It's too late to change what's happened,' she said wearily. 'Perhaps if I spoke to Vigadó, or if we could think of some logical approach——'

'Dammit, Suzanne!' he roared. 'Do you think I haven't tried every avenue? I've done everything. I've thought of every angle. I've lain awake at night, thinking, thinking, till my brains have bled!' He took her by the arms and shook her violently, his temper all but snapped. 'You and your damn prim English morals! Go along with my idea! Pretend you're sleeping with me—or do so; do it—since it's what we both want! Refuse and you destroy my family! Have you no heart?'

'Oh, please,' she whispered, swaying in his cruel grip. 'You could destroy *my* family!'

'Temporarily! Whereas mine... They'd be scarred for life. Do you know what this will do to Dinah?' he snarled savagely. 'She might seem strong and capable but only because Jo and I give her security. If I fall, the business crashes and so will Jo as my right-hand man. She will be left to hold the family together on her own. Lara. Nikki——'

'You made me like them! You made me enjoy being with them! You brute! Please don't do this to me!' she begged brokenly.

'I have to,' he said grimly. 'I don't think you have any idea of the threads I hold securely in my hand. If I go under, millions of people throughout the world will become bankrupt or lose their businesses. Some will commit suicide. The consequences of my failure are vast. *That* is my responsibility in life. That's why I'd never commit fraud, because I could never live with the repercussions. I carry the lives of countless other people on my shoulders, as well as the future of my own children.'

'Oh, God!' she moaned. She felt powerless. Her well-ordered, organised life had been shattered by him. He'd drawn her into his complex world where one undone stitch could unravel everything.

The loathing in his eyes made her cringe. 'And despite all I've told you, you still hesitate! You won't pretend to be in love with me because it's untrue!' He drew in a breath, so emotionally wound up that he seemed close to erupting at any moment. 'If you don't support me now, and my world falls apart, I swear to God that I'll see you and every one of your family in the flames of eternal damnation before I go under!'

'I can't think!' she wailed. 'Why did you tell me all this? How can I concentrate with all this turmoil in my mind, going round and round and getting nowhere?'

'Now,' he grated, 'you know how I feel.'

'I don't know what to do. I honestly don't,' she sobbed.

And after coldly watching her howling in abject misery for a while, suddenly he drew her close, sheltering her in his strong arms while she cried till she thought her heart would break. Weak and limp with exhaustion, she made no protest when he walked her up the path and collected her handbag from the kitchen where she'd left it. She hardly noticed that they were in his car and driving off into the night, with László muttering furiously into a car phone. It was only when they were walking towards a small jet plane that she shrank back and refused to go any further.

'I'm taking you home,' he said grimly. 'Then you can think all you like.'

'Home?' she asked blankly.

'Devon.'

Home, she thought, instantly comforted. There she could find something normal in her life again.

In silence they boarded the plane. Some time later—she had no idea how long—they had landed in Exeter, hired a car, and she'd been deposited in the lane outside her beloved family home. He turned the key in the door for her and she noticed his hand was shaking. Without a word, he pushed open the door and switched on the light, listened for a moment and stepped back.

'Goodbye.'

'László!' she cried in bewilderment. He ignored her and strode back to the hire car. She ran to the gate. 'What do you mean, goodbye?'

'I have a feeling I'm going to have to shoulder this problem on my own,' he said, and in his voice was an exhaustion and a defeat that she'd never heard before.

That affected her deeply. He'd always been so strong, so invincible. Now he needed her, his family threatened, his whole life in jeopardy, and she was letting him down.

'Just a moment,' she said. Choices, she thought. Like the countess, who'd weighed up two alternatives and had chosen the one which would do the most good. But——

'I can't hang around here while you weigh up the pros and cons,' László said irritably. 'Do it in your own time. I think I know your answer. Goodbye, Suzanne.'

She watched him walk slowly to the car and she felt terror. Without him, she couldn't be happy. Somehow she had to stop him, even if for a night...

'Don't go!' she pleaded. 'There's—there's no one here. Father's still with the countess at the castle. You can't leave me here alone——'

'Watch.'

She bit her lip, desperate to stop him. Never to see him again! Her heart missed a beat. She loved him! He couldn't go. 'Stay,' she croaked.

'There's nothing to stay for,' he muttered.

'Me?' Without thinking of the consequences, she said in a rush, 'I want you to spend the night with me!'

She saw his step falter, then he continued. One night, she thought. To know him, to really be part of him for one night, was all she asked. In panic, she ran around the car and pushed him against it, flinging her arms up and pulling his head down hard, her lips driving into his. And kissed him again and again, because he'd remained immobile, while she pleaded silently for his animal lust to surface just this once.

'No, Suzanne,' he muttered roughly, tearing his mouth away.

'I—I love you!' she cried, shocking them both.

'No,' he said harshly.

'Yes, I do!' she insisted.

'*No!*'

Glaring at him, she stripped off her cotton jacket. 'I do,' she muttered ominously.

'You can't! Don't be ridiculous,' he scorned. 'A woman like you, from a tin-pot village in the English countryside? I'm a bastard. A liar, a cheat——'

'It's not tin-pot! It's God's little acre!' she yelled, and flicked back her hair and scowled at him from under her lashes, yanking open the buttons of her blouse.

'—too old for you, father of two——'

And, impatient to seduce him, she ripped the last few buttons away and triumphantly revealed her trembling body.

László gulped visibly, his eyes transfixed by the swell of her pale breasts above the half-cup bra. '—grandfather...'

'You're running out of excuses,' she muttered in satisfaction.

'I know,' he said thickly, mesmerised by the way she lifted her hair off her neck. 'Suzanne——'

'This is how I love you,' she said softly, her finger touching his parted lips. 'This is how I trust you.'

'I can't,' he whispered, suckling her finger.

'Touch me,' she murmured dreamily.

'No,' he husked. She let her body slide against his, her eyes flirting with him, her lashes thick and fluttering. 'Please, don't . . . oh, God, you're so beautiful! I—no, don't, damn you, don't . . .'

'I know what I'm doing,' she said lovingly. 'I will do what you want and beg Vigadó and Mariann to hear everything you have to say. I'll support your cause. You need me. Take what you want, take everything you need. Tell them I'm your mistress. Say we're getting married. Tell Vigadó you'll walk out of——' she stumbled over the dreadful words. 'Out of . . . my life,' she whispered, 'if he'll cancel publication of the book.' She swallowed. He'd leave her. She was digging her own grave. But the children and his reputation would be safe and justice would be done. What else could she do? She loved him so much.

He held her tightly, wrapping her in arms of steel, kissing her hair, her forehead, her neck, mouth . . .

Hours—minutes—seconds later, when she shivered, he slowly unwound her arms. One from where it stretched to the smooth, warm flesh of his back beneath his shirt, the other . . . she blushed and hastily snatched it from the hollow inside his hipbone. Her body felt as though he had kissed every inch—which he almost had. And despite the worries they had to face, she felt strangely at peace because they were together for the time being. She put aside the pain she'd suffer later. She knew that he was staying with her for two reasons; because he needed her to stop the book publication and because he lusted after her. When those two needs had been satisfied, he'd go.

She swayed, feeling dizzy.

'You're tired,' he said huskily. 'Tired and cold. I am not making love to you tonight.'

'Why?' she mumbled, almost asleep on her feet.

He chuckled. 'Because you're so tired you wouldn't be any good,' he said drily. 'We're going to have a hot drink—or something viciously alcoholic, or both—and sleep alone. Then——'

'Then in the morning we're returning to Hungary,' she said shakily.

'You'll do what I ask?' he asked, his eyes narrowed with caution.

'Yes. I will.'

They lingered in the morning, because Widecombe-in-the-Moor was looking at its most beautiful. She took him to her favourite spot where they could see for miles; the undulating moorland a sharp green against the cornflower sky and Widecombe's soaring church tower a lasting monument to the tin miners who paid for it to be built. England at its best, gentle, lush, soothing.

'God, it's beautiful!' he murmured in awe. 'No wonder you love it so much. I feel . . . I feel there's space here.' His eyes rested on the wild ponies, galloping for sheer joy across the open hills. 'Space to breathe. Silence. Only larks, and swallows and the sound of the river.'

Suzanne's heart filled with emotion. 'I'm so glad you appreciate it,' she said huskily, her face uplifted to his. He seemed at peace, the early morning sun softening the harshness of his profile.

'I could be so happy here,' he said softly.

'I love you,' she said, overflowing with tenderness and the poignant knowledge that she would remember this moment for a long time and come here alone, to think of what might have been.

His chin lifted and she could see that he clenched his jaw and that his eyes brooded on the square patch of graveyard on the slope of the hill. 'We must go.'

Tears pricking her eyes, she nodded and prepared for the journey. When they landed a short time after lunch, László telephoned to check that Vigadó would be at home and discovered he was with the countess at the castle.

Suzanne felt nerves crawling in her stomach as they came up the drive. She knew what she had to do: to persuade everyone that she worshipped the ground that László walked on. It was so true that she feared she'd alienate her family for ever—and that when he left her, she'd have no one left to turn to, no one to comfort her.

'Oh, Countess!' she cried shakily, running into the woman's outstretched, welcoming arms. 'Where—where's Mariann?'

'I'm glad to see you at last. We thought you were deliberately staying away from us, child!' complained the countess. 'And Mariann's stuck in Belgrade. Good morning, Mr Lázár.'

'Countess Ana. We've come to see Vigadó,' he said stiffly, his skin taut over the high bones.

'You'll see me first.'

And the countess regally drew Suzanne towards the study. Politeness stopped her from jerking away, but she cast a frantic look at the thunderous László and he gritted his teeth and followed.

'I don't want to see you,' he muttered to his mother. 'I have business with Vigadó——'

'Your business might be a little easier to carry out once you've heard what I have to say,' Ana said quietly. 'You see, we were all worried about Suzanne's association with you——'

'I love him!' cried Suzanne fervently, linking her arm with László's.

'That's obvious from your letters,' said Ana gently. 'So I did a little checking up on him.' He stiffened and made to speak, but she lifted a hand and he waited, silent and suspicious. 'We all find it difficult to make sense of what I've discovered,' went on the countess gravely. She glanced at some papers on the desk. 'I see that you're involved in the promotion of women's rights and have made heavy commitments of your precious time to the Human Rights movement. You co-ordinate European and American investment in Hungary and in the Eastern Bloc states——'

'How did you discover that?' he demanded with a faint frown.

'I am the Countess Ana Huszár,' she said proudly. 'I have links with everyone.' She looked quizzical. 'And it seems you are something of a secret philanthropist, Mr Lázár, creating foundations, funding youth projects and generally acting like a saint,' she said, with a humourous twist to her mouth. 'A man to be admired. How you acquired the bad reputation several people—including my son—accuse you of, I don't know.'

Suzanne felt hope surge in her. 'He is a good man!' she cried fervently. 'He's not as evil as he's been painted! If you saw him with his children——'

'I've read all about that with some surprise. It was your letters to Mariann,' said the countess gently, 'that alarmed us. Your László seemed to be a different person in your eyes; someone who was gentle and just, honest and tender. And Mariann swore that you were wise and sensible and not easily led. She told us how she respected your judgement, that you were level-headed and could analyse a situation better than anyone.'

'Oh!' Suzanne said weakly.

'In fact, we all thought this to be true and that you wouldn't ally yourself with a monster, even for love, which doesn't often give us wise choices in our partners. Your principles are too high and you have too strong and passionate a duty to the family you love. So that is why I decided to investigate thoroughly, to dig deep and to find out the truth. I must confess, Mr Lázár,' she said thoughtfully, 'if you hadn't behaved so atrociously towards my son, I would have been eager to become better acquainted with you.'

'Well I'll be damned!' murmured László. Suzanne clutched at his hand and he smiled down on her in delight.

'Not this time, I think,' smiled the countess. 'Vigadó has decided to postpone publication until you have time to talk to one another——'

'László isn't a crook!' insisted Suzanne. 'He's been framed. We can tell Vigadó everything—he'll understand, I know he will, he must!'

'I'm sure he will, he as much as said so, when I presented him with the evidence,' said the countess reassuringly. 'Apart from the overwhelming evidence of Suzanne's approval, there's plenty of other evidence in your favour, László—and I think Vigadó would be the first to agree that guilt by implication is unfair. He had the same trouble with his less-than-honest father-in-law,' she said with a chuckle, 'and he was incorrectly branded a corrupt businessman himself. I think that once he's been given the evidence I have that he'll burn the manuscript and cut his losses.'

'Ohhh, Countess!' Suzanne ran to the woman and hugged her tightly. 'You've made me so happy,' she said passionately.

'I am indebted to you, Countess,' said László huskily.

Something in his tone made Suzanne detach herself and turn around. He was looking at his mother in a strange, frightening way and she felt the blood in her veins turn to ice. 'No, László!' she moaned. 'You can't!'

'My family is safe,' he said softly. 'I have nothing to lose. Countess, there was a reason why I tried to make István's restoration of the estate as difficult as possible—— '

'No!' wailed Suzanne. 'Please, don't say it! Don't tell her!'

'Oh, Suzanne,' he said gently. 'Don't you see that the situation has changed dramatically?'

'Yes,' she moaned. 'And you——'

'And I can tell you how deeply I love you!' he said shakily.

She froze. It was a trick. He was making her weak so that he could plunge knives into her heart and make his vengeful announcement to the countess. But... His face told another story. It looked...loving. Tender. Her heart lurched. 'László——'

'My darling,' he said huskily. 'I couldn't bear putting you through the mill any longer. It's hurt me beyond belief to torment you. It hurt me to deny myself the pleasure of saying how I felt about you, that for some time I've loved you very, very deeply. That's why I took you home yesterday—because I couldn't bear to tear you apart any more—and then, like a crazy fool, like some teenage kid with a crush, I couldn't bear leaving you! I wanted an excuse, anything, to keep us together for as long as possible——'

'László!' she cried, her voice trembling with joy, 'you fool, you fool, don't you know that's exactly how I felt too? I decided that I'd do anything to keep us together, anything at all!'

He strode over and took her in his arms and she gazed up at him, hardly seeing his face because there was a veil of happy tears in her eyes. 'You will marry me,' he said, and laughed. 'You won't break our engagement?'

'Marry you!' she said dreamily. 'Oh, my darling
László, everything will be all right now. We'll talk to my
family and explain.'

'You little witch,' he murmured affectionately, 'I did
everything I could *not* to fall in love with you, and you
wove your way into my affections despite all my efforts!'

Her head was spinning. He loved her. Nothing else
mattered. 'Oh, László!' she whispered. 'When I thought
I'd never see you again, I felt as though the world had
come to an end! It's right: it's only when you're about
to lose something precious that you realise just how important it is to you.'

She saw his longing eyes go to the countess and felt
the ache in his heart repeated within her. But dared not
speak the words that hovered on her lips: Countess, this
is your son.

'When you marry, I hope you'll live near to us all,'
smiled the countess warmly. 'Your sisters will love that.'

'Oh.' Suzanne's face grew solemn. She'd had no time
to give that any thought. They'd live in Hungary or
Russia, or New York...

László tipped up her reluctant chin. 'Your business
will be based in Devon as you planned,' he said quietly.
'On the way here I was thinking and wishing——' He
smiled. 'I see no reason why our dreams can't come true.
I'll tell you mine. That in between rushing around the
world with you and visiting Dinah and family and your
family here, we will live in Devon too. In Widecombe,
where we can ride on the moors and walk for miles
without seeing a soul, where the peace and beauty will
make a good home for our children and for us. I'd like
that to be our home. I've never wanted a home before;
now I do, and I want to be there, where you are happy.'

'I can't tell you how much I love you,' she said simply.
Her eyes told the rest.

'I'm so very happy for you both,' said the countess
fondly, and kissed them both. Her eyes lingered on
László, seeing the yearning within them, and something
must have registered within her because she said in a
trembling voice, 'I feel as though I know you. I look
into your eyes and...' She gave a small, embarrassed
laugh. 'I see nothing but good in you,' she said. 'You

must explain your hostility to my son, because I want us all to be a close-knit and loving family and for us all to visit you in your home.'

László looked visibly shaken. 'There is another home where we could have lived,' he said softly, 'but it belongs to someone else—not legally, but morally.' He gently lifted Suzanne's hand and kissed it. 'You don't mind not being a countess, do you, darling?' he asked fondly.

'No!' she cried passionately. 'Oh, László, you're giving the castle to István!'

'And I'm giving my mother a gift,' he said gently. They both laughed at the countess's puzzled expression. 'I'm giving her a son, and I'm giving her a new daughter-in-law.' His dark eyes glowed. 'You lied to Suzanne,' he said quietly to the countess. 'There was a baby born here. Your son. Nikolai Romanov's son.'

The countess blanched and she staggered a little before recovering her balance by gripping the edge of the desk. 'You know about him?' She leaned into the desk and covered her face with her hands. 'I tried to forget,' she moaned. 'My child . . . my little boy . . . Nikolai took him away from me! Oh, Suzanne,' she sobbed, when Suzanne's arms went around her in sympathy, 'he said I wasn't fit to care for him because I was a Hungarian! And I loved him—he was all I had in the world to love, and I'd cherished him and talked to him all the time I carried him . . . and Nikolai took him. I never forgave him after that!' she said bitterly. 'And my baby died without ever knowing how much I loved him——'

'No,' growled László, his voice thick with emotion. He held the two tearful women. 'He didn't die. It's me, Mother. Your son.'

His rough words cracked like broken glass. Suzanne felt the countess become still, saw her tear-spattered face lift in hope and fear and stare at the single tear that glistened on László's cheek.

'My . . . son? My László?'

Suzanne left them together, her heart too full to cope with their reunion. For a long while, after speaking to Vigadó, she sat in the window of the romantic castle, her mind calm and at peace. László loved her. And their families wouldn't be at loggerheads any more. She heard the door open gently and then close. His well-loved arms came around her and she leaned against his chest.

'She loved me,' he said softly. 'My father had lied to me to stop me caring for her, to prevent me from seeking her out and having to choose between them; between Hungary and Russia. He was misguided. But I understand. Life is nothing but choices.'

She slipped under his arms and stood up, lifting her hands to touch his loving face. A smile softened her lips and he kissed her smile, drawing her into a long, tender embrace. Eventually she leaned back and thoughtfully stroked the silver streaks of hair behind his ears.

'Did your mother have a fit to discover that in one day she'd acquired a son, a grandchild and a great-grandchild?' she asked with a laugh.

'She's on the phone,' he grinned indulgently, 'the line's red-hot and I think she'll be talking for hours, telling all her friends.'

'I'm afraid the Evans girls have done something dreadfully complicated to the Huszár dynasty and its family tree!' she giggled. 'We ought to tell your children——'

'They can wait,' he husked, nuzzling her throat. 'First, we're having a quiet, uneventful week to ourselves. In Widecombe.'

'Uneventful?' she pouted.

He kissed the pout, as she hoped he would. 'Not...entirely,' he murmured, and gave a ragged sigh when she moved against him invitingly. 'I don't think I can wait till Widecombe,' he whispered. And led her into the garden, to the lake. He picked roses, strewing the petals on the grass and then lay her with great tenderness and love on the perfumed carpet.

'I've not made love to a grandpa before,' she mumbled, her mouth moving over his smooth, golden shoulder.

'Grandpa be damned!' he muttered roughly, and crushed her in his powerful, muscular arms.

HARLEQUIN PRESENTS®

The latest in our tantalizing new selection of stories...

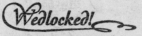

Bonded in matrimony, torn by desire...

Next month watch for:

***Ruthless Contract* by Kathryn Ross**
Harlequin Presents #1807

Locked in a loveless marriage. Abbie and Greg were
prepared to sacrifice their freedom to give Abbie's adorable
nieces a stable home...but were determined that their
emotions wouldn't be involved.

Then fate stepped in and played her final card, and
the ruthless contract between Abbie and Greg became a
contract for passion.

Available in April wherever Harlequin books are sold.